## There Was Somebody Crouched Down in Front of the Safe . . .

All I could see was a hat and the impression of eyeglasses flashing dully in the light of the lantern as whoever it was turned around when he felt the draft from the open door.

"Hey," I said. All I got out was the first word because the lantern was picked up and swung at my head as somebody big and bulky tried to go right through me on the way to the door. I ducked but managed to get hold of a piece of mackinaw, enough to send the intruder sprawling but not enough to hold on to, as I went down. The light of the lantern went out. We both scrambled to our feet at the same time. I started moving forward when something flashed. There was a crack like a tree limb snapping off on a bitter cold night and I felt a sting on the side of my face that knocked me sideways.

Then the shadow was gone. I reached for the light switch as a car pulled up outside, its _____'s spraying gravel.

"Hey, you!" I heard so_____ you! Stop in the name _____ ice old-fashioned t_____ en. The metal box_____ too. A deputy, bundled_____ es, and a hat with ear flaps, ap_____ oorway.

"You must be Jake _____, he said. He walked up to me and gently pulled my hand away from my ear. "Somebody clipped off your earlobe."

# Robert Campbell

# PLUGGED NICKEL

**POCKET BOOKS**

New York   London   Toronto   Sydney   Tokyo

This novel is a work of fiction. Names, characters, places and incidents are either the product of the author's imagination or are used fictitiously. Any resemblance to actual events or locales or persons, living or dead, is entirely coincidental.

Another *Original* publication of POCKET BOOKS

POCKET BOOKS, a division of Simon & Schuster, Inc.
1230 Avenue of the Americas, New York, N.Y. 10020

ISBN: 0-671-64363-0

First Pocket Books printing March 1988

10 9 8 7 6 5 4 3 2 1

POCKET and colophon are trademarks of Simon & Schuster, Inc.

Printed in the U.S.A.

# PLUGGED NICKEL

# One

IT WAS FOUR-TWENTY IN the A.M. The rain was beating down like it wanted to flood the world. The California Zephyr out of Chicago, on the way to San Francisco/Oakland, was crawling around a sharp curve along the tracks of the Burlington Northern through an almost uninhabited, lonely stretch of road about twenty-five minutes outside McCook, Nebraska, thirty-five minutes away from Akron, Colorado, on the way to Denver.

The whole train was asleep, the high rollers in the roomettes and compartments all tucked in, the working folks making do with the reclining chairs in coach, the railroad personnel asleep in the dormitory car, the few on duty dozing off sitting up but ready to respond if called.

I was awake, looking at my face in the mirror created by the night outside the rain-streaked window. The runnels on the glass scarred the image, making me look twice my age. Which was about how old I felt. My eyes were burning, my feet hurt, and my collar felt tight even though the top button was undone.

*For God's sake, I probably had high blood pressure, the beginnings of varicose veins, and for sure, I needed glasses.*

I'm a railroad plainclothes cop working for Burlington Northern out of the Omaha office. I was aboard because it was me who caught the call from the station agent at Ottumwa, Iowa, the night before, warning us about some surly types that, in his opinion, might be riding on stolen tickets. So, at 10:45 P.M. I'd swung aboard and found out within fifteen minutes that the "surly types" were Baptist ministers on their way to some convention in Salt Lake City.

I could've gotten off at Lincoln, Nebraska, around midnight, kipped down in the station, and caught the eastbound Zephyr back to Omaha around 5:30 A.M., but I decided I might as well go on to Fort Morgan, Colorado. I'd arrive there just about the same time. I have a friend, Janel Butterfield, lives just off the main highway about fifteen miles outside of Fort Morgan. If I could catch or beg a ride that early in the morning, I could be sitting down to one of Janel's country breakfasts around 6:30.

I should've gotten off and gone home to Omaha. Then I wouldn't've become involved and had the bottom of my left ear shot off.

Anyway, I was looking at my reflection, convincing myself I wasn't such a bad-looking fella after all, when the brakes grabbed the tracks, squealing like two hundred scalded cats and almost pushing me up-standing out of my seat.

People were awake, mumbling, coughing, and complaining all over the coach. Right away I started thinking about what a miracle it would be if some sleeping passenger hadn't been dumped out of his or her chair or bed so hard that the road would be getting sued from one end of the line to the other.

I grabbed my shearling coat and hat out of the overhead and hurried down the aisle to the end of the car, walking through three of them before spotting Halt Ennery, the conductor. He had his black rubber rain cape slung around his shoulders, his cap on his head, and a lantern in his hand. He was just sliding the door in the middle of the coach aside, apologizing to the passengers for letting the storm blow in on their blanket-covered legs, when I hurried up and asked what was going on.

Being a train conductor is like being the captain of a seagoing vessel. Whatever out of the ordinary needs doing he ends up doing. Halt laid the lantern down, sat on the floor, turned around, and slid his legs over the side, looking up at me with a woeful glance that said he was too old to be dropping God-knew-how-far into God-knew-what on a dark night full of driving rain. He dangled out there, thrashing his legs around until he found some footing, then let go. I handed him his lantern, felt in my pocket for my own six-cell flashlight, and followed him through the door. Going out in that storm was like walking face-first into a hail of carpet tacks.

"What happened?" I shouted, hoping for better results the second time I asked.

"Somebody pulled the emergency."

"Is that all you know?"

"If I knew any more, Jake, you think I'd be going out in this goddamn stuff?" he shouted back. "Watch yourself, the road falls off steep along here."

The roadbed had been built along a rocky ridge that ran through a stretch of wooded mountain that was beautiful when seen by day but was a hellish place at night in the driving rain. It fell off on both sides, one side a lot more than the other. I could hear rushing water, way down below off to my left, above the sound of the wind in the pines and the rain slashing cross-wise across the land. The beam of my flashlight couldn't even reach the cut where the white water roared.

If a person slipped down that embankment and didn't get caught lucky by some scraggly bush or twisted root, they'd end up in that rage of water and get tossed out somewhere on the other side of the Rockies.

Starting to walk back toward the rear of the train, I saw Laws Ruskel, one of the two brakemen, hurrying along the ties, his red-faced lantern swaying like the tip of a wire-walker's balancing pole.

I glanced back and could just about make out Halt trudging away from me, but I couldn't see anybody coming down the road from the engine end. Charlie Tichenor, the engineer, would stay in his cab, but Billy Turk, who tended the boilers, might have decided to come out and see what was up. If he had, he was out of my sight on the other side of the train like the other brakeman would be.

Steam was pouring out of the discharge valves,

spilling up off the roadbed like the heavy, lazy fog of dry ice around an ice cream freezer. I found myself wishing it was summer and Janel and me were off to the fair grounds for a picnic feed.

"You better watch where you're walking," Laws yelled, just as I stumbled over something. I was about to turn around to give him hell for startling me and almost making me fall, when I looked down where the flashlight beam was cutting through the rain and saw the leg and foot. It looked almost foolish lying there, a leg in dark pants, black with rain, a foot wearing a white sock and a black shoe.

I moved the flash and saw the other leg and foot. Laws came up to me.

"Oh, my god," he said. "Should we try to get him out from under there?"

"I don't really know," I said, my heart pounding in my neck like to choke me. "If he's still alive but bad hurt, moving him can do nothing but harm."

While we went dithering on about it, Billy let out a yell from about a car length along the other side of the train. "I found something. Oh, dear Christ!"

Billy wasn't given to such expressions of dismay, so this last remark was enough to make us run down to where the train was between him and us. We squatted down and I shone my flash under the carriage, hoping to get a look at whatever it was Billy was carrying on about.

"There's *half* of somebody laying on the track over here," Billy shouted.

There was a mangled mess on the rails and ties just about where the victim's belt should've been. There was nothing below it. Just a torso with the battered

11

head turned aside and the arms flung out as though impaled on the tracks. It was a sight I'd rather not have seen.

Laws saw it too and promptly turned away to leave his dinner on the side of the roadbed. I held on, watching him as he turned his face up to the rain and opened his mouth to wash it out. Then he wiped his face in the crook of his arm.

I ran like hell back to the legs we'd found, Laws stumbling along behind me. I hunkered down with the flash and took a look at the condition of our discovery. I was looking at the other half. Up close, it surprised me that there wasn't more of a mess than you'd expect.

*Once I was there when a track worker had lost his leg under a train. The tremendous weight of the engine had sealed off the ends of the arteries and veins and it hadn't been near as bloody as I would've guessed.*

"Well, don't worry about it," I shouted back to Billy. "We got the other half on our side."

"What do you think we ought to do?" Laws said.

"Well, it wouldn't hurt to introduce them," I said.

It was a hell of a thing to say, making light of a horrible tragedy like that, but anybody who's been around death much, or even at all, knows that people do things like that.

I told Laws to go get some tarps from somewhere, and bent down to pull my half of the poor bastard out from under the train.

# Two

HALT ENNERY IS A very serious sort of fellow. If you asked him was the sun shining, he'd squint up at it until the tears came, get a five-minute sunburn, and then tell you he'd have to take your question under advisement. There's not a better man to have around, whether it's trailing through new country on a fishing trip or building an outhouse the cheapest way possible, as long as there's a book to go by. Without a set of directions, though, Halt has a hard time tying his shoelaces.

Laws Ruskel, on the other hand, is the sort of man will shoot the horse first and find out why it went lame after.

Billy Turk is hard of hearing when he wants to be, and doesn't say much of anything, except when nothing else will move the train.

13

So, all four of us, plus Harry Bishop, the other brakeman, were standing out there in the rain, gathered around the lower part of the corpse, now covered with a tarp, deciding what to do. Laws'd brought a stretcher along with the tarps. Seeing it laying on the ground next to the ruined body gave me a very funny feeling.

I was also aware that several passengers, rumpled with sleep, were peering out of the car windows with the curiosity of raccoons pinching up their mouths and squinting up their eyes, not seeing much but getting testy about the long delay.

"I say let's toss the two pieces into the baggage car and get the hell on our way," Laws said, cocky now that he was over being sick.

"Can't do it," Halt said. "According to regulations, this train can't move until the coroner gets here and declares this fellow dead."

"I don't want to get picky about it," Laws said, "but anybody can't take one look and tell this fella's dead, ain't never seen dead."

" 'Any bodies found along the right of way are to remain untouched until the proper authorities arrive to determine cause and circumstance.' I'm not sure we even did the right thing getting those pieces out from under the wheels," Halt insisted.

"It also says that any obstruction or hazard along or beside the track or roadbed is to be cleared away expeditiously," Laws said.

"I think they had trees or rocks in mind," Halt replied.

"I don't think it's up to us to decide what was

meant," Laws came back. "An obstruction is an obstruction, and a hazard is a hazard."

Billy stood there in the wet sucking on his pipe. It amazed me how he even got the thing lit in the pouring rain, but Billy does things like that all the time, amazing people who've known him for twenty years. He was looking at me as though he expected I should say something.

*I apply a rule to myself: not to open my mouth until everybody else has chewed the bone. I've also learned it's always best to let somebody else remind those assembled that I'm a law officer and that I'm on the scene.*

"Jake, here"—Billy finally spoke up, when I wouldn't—"for the lack of any other authorized person, is the legal representative of the commonwealth."

"Oh, for the good Lord's sake, Billy, what's that supposed to mean?" Laws complained.

Billy looked at me again, tossing me the baby so to speak. His look told me that so far as he was concerned it was now up to me to say what was what and if I wanted to drop the baby in the mud that was all right with him too.

"Billy's just reminding us," I said, "that I'm a duly constituted officer of the law."

"Put it away," Halt said smartly. "This train don't move until the coroner gets here."

"We don't even know what county we're in," Laws said.

"I know," Halt said. "We're in Washington County. Akron's the next stop."

"Seventeen hundred people in that town. You think

it's even got a coroner? Maybe we should take the body back to McCook."

"We're not in Nebraska, we're in Colorado. Akron's the county seat and the county's got to have a coroner."

"Probably the druggist," Laws said.

"I don't care if it's the hairdresser. All I want is somebody official to point his finger at that body and declare it dead, so we can get on with it," Halt said, then turned his back and started walking toward the cab, obviously intending to get on the radiophone and call dispatch.

"Halt," I called out.

He turned around.

"Since we already moved the parts off the tracks," I said, "I don't suppose it would do any harm to get the fella put back together and on the stretcher. It would be the decent thing to do."

I think he nodded as he walked on. At least he didn't say no.

"He's very stubborn," Laws said.

"He's doing what he thinks is right," I said. "And maybe he *is* right. There could be a lot of fuss about jurisdiction on this one. I mean people getting hit along the railroad right of way always causes confusion about where and when it happened and who's to take responsibility for the investigation. Could be up to Amtrak. Could be up to Burlington Northern. Could be up to the county sheriff's office or the state police. Being that it happened along the route of an interstate carrier, it could even be the FBI'll want to take over. So, there's no sense in putting a foot wrong if we can help it."

The train moved ahead far enough for us to cross the tracks. The beam from my flashlight showed a wide, brush-filled gully not too far below the roadbed off to the right, not a tenth as steep or far as the fall down to the river.

We gathered up the top half of the dead man. It was a hard, sad piece of work. The rain let up some.

# Three

WHEN WE GOT THE two pieces together on a stretcher, I decided to do something instead of standing there with my finger in my ear. I could've left it all alone, but I was hoping to find something that'd tell me if he'd been on the train or walking the tracks. Some identification that would allow me to check among the passengers and maybe find someone who was wondering where their father, brother, husband, or boyfriend had up and gone to.

I stooped down and pulled the tarp away from the head and torso. One side of the face had been badly damaged, the other had not. He looked to be a fair-skinned man with light hair darkened by the rain. About fifty years of age.

I started going through his pockets, replacing what I found as I went along.

There was a pair of unbroken spectacles in the

outside breast pocket of the jacket, three soggy cork-tipped cigarette butts in one side pocket, and a crumpled package of Fritos in the other. One of the inside pockets had a railroad timetable in it. The other was empty.

I covered up the top half and uncovered the bottom. The left-hand slash pocket had a handkerchief with something that, under the beam of the flashlight, looked like a smudge of lipstick; the right-hand one some change and a money clip holding some bills. I didn't count either. There were no keys.

"Who wants to give me a hand here?" I said.

"A hand doing what?" Laws asked.

"I've got to get to the back pockets of his trousers and somebody's got to tip him a little."

"Oh," Laws said, but didn't make a move. Neither did Billy, but that could've been because he hadn't heard what was wanted.

Bishop squatted down beside me.

He's a big, pale, dependable man who's always very obliging and as a rule says even less than Billy.

He put his hands under the corpse's thigh and rolled him over so I could get to the left-hand back pocket. There was only an extra-large comb in it. Then he reached across and tilted the body the other way, toward him. The right-hand pocket had a little book in it.

It was almost dry, having been protected from the rain by the victim's own body, then the train car, then the tarp. It was a book of poems with the place marked with a train ticket from Denver to Chicago.

*He'd been riding a train going the wrong way.*

"So, we know he wasn't walking the tracks," I said,

putting the book in my own pocket so it wouldn't get wet and ruined.

"Now all we've got to do is find out how and why he got off the train while it was moving," Laws said.

"Well, I'm going back inside," I said. "Come with me, will you, Billy?"

"I'm going inside too," Laws said.

"Somebody's got to stay out here with the body," I said.

"Who the hell's going to steal it?" Laws said.

"Rain could come down hard again and wash a piece of it down into the ravine. Wild animals could come along. . . ."

"Rain washes it down, I ain't going to get washed down with it," Laws said, "and I doubt there's any animals out on a night like this. Creatures are too sensible to stand out in the open and drown."

Bishop sort of gave a big sigh and hunkered down close to the side of the car, his poncho around his shoulders, looking like some old Indian waking the dead.

# Four

THE RADIOPHONE ON A train is not your corner telephone box. You can't decide to call home en route and tell the wife to hold supper because the train's a half hour late.

The frequency ties the train to a dispatcher who could be some distance away. In this case the dispatcher was in Denver. Halt would probably have to rouse him out of bed and ask him to call the county coroner in Akron on the regular telephone. Tell him he was wanted with an ambulance along the Burlington Northern right of way about midway between Akron and McCook. Report back to the train that help was coming. Then hope coroner and ambulance would arrive as promised.

I had a lot of doubts about whether the coroner would be willing to come out to the middle of nowhere on a stormy night along whatever pitch-dark road might get him there. As far as I knew, there was no vehicular road that paralleled the railroad tracks along this section. There'd be country and mountain roads at crossings, but how far away the nearest one might be was something I'd have to let Halt worry about.

My immediate concern, as I told Billy as soon as I got him alone for a minute inside the first coach, was to find out what I could about what stopped the train. Somebody had pulled the emergency and it would go a long way to finding out what'd happened to the dead man if I could discover who that somebody might be.

*Except I doubted if anybody would come forward.*

"What are we pulling, Billy?" I said.

"Four coaches, two sleepers, baggage, diner, lounge, and dorm. We've also got a deadhead."

"Head or tail?"

"Up ahead, behind the engines."

I did a quick calculation in my head.

The Burlington Northern crew would be composed of Halt Ennery, Charlie Tichenor, and Billy Turk, the two brakemen, Laws Ruskel and Harry Bishop, and depending on the amount of mail, one or two men in baggage. If the coach seats in the upper deck of the dormitory car were sold, Burlington Northern would have one of their employees attending that car. So, say six on the low end and eight on the high end.

This crew would be changed for a Denver and Rio Grande Western crew in Denver. I'd have a reasonable chance to talk to them about their impressions, if any, once we got there. So, I could put that part of what I figured I had to do on hold.

There was one attendant to each coach and sleeper

car and five in the diner. These eleven people were Amtrak and stayed aboard for the whole trip from Chicago to San Francisco/Oakland. That was how come the dormitory car.

What concerned me at the moment were the passengers.

I could take names and addresses, but there was no way I could make them stay aboard when we finally got moving again and pulled into the Akron station and stations west.

"I can't question every one of them, either," I told Billy, "even if we stayed here a day or two, and I hope to God that doesn't happen. There's seventy-two people in each coach and I don't know how many in each sleeper. I could never cover the ground.

"So, what I'm going to do is this. I'm going to make an announcement in each of the coaches. In the lounge car and the diner too, if Halt opens them up. I want you to stand next to me and keep your eyes open."

"What am I looking for, Jake?"

"I haven't got the vaguest. I'm going to state the case in each car. I'm going to ask if anybody's missing or if anybody pulled the emergency. I'm going to ask them if they saw anybody else do it."

"So, I'm looking for a twitch?"

"A twitch. A shifty eye. A guilty flush."

"You're asking a lot."

"What else have I got?"

I called for attention in the first coach.

"Ladies and gentlemen, we're very sorry to inconvenience you this way," I said loud enough for every-

23

body to hear. "There's been an accident. Somebody's been hit along the right of way. It appears he was a passenger who somehow jumped or fell off this train."

I let them digest that while they rubbed a little more sleep out of their eyes.

"I'm a police officer for the Burlington Northern Railroad. Until I'm told differently, I'm going to conduct an investigation. You can understand, the sooner you can get impressions about a thing like this, the better off you are. That doesn't mean that other law enforcement representatives won't be after you to answer questions later on."

They had a little discussion among themselves about the inconvenience this might cost them down the line.

"First, I'd like to know if one of you is traveling with someone that's gone somewhere and not come back before or since the train stopped?" When nobody spoke up, I went on, "In that case I'd like to know if anybody saw anything that made you pull the emergency cord?"

Just like I figured, no one admitted to committing such an act. There were a lot of murmurs about being asleep and being practically knocked down on the floor when the brakes were applied, some people already working up their stories in case they decided to sue, but nothing about pulling the cord or seeing anybody else pull it.

"The next question naturally follows," I went on. "Did anyone see anybody *else* pull the emergency?"

They didn't disappoint me. Nobody'd seen a thing. Everybody'd been asleep.

"Did you notice anything or anybody that struck

you as odd or out of the ordinary earlier in the night or evening? Anything at all. It might be something very small. Something you might have thought about and then decided right away was silly. If there's anything like that, I'm going to be back in the dining car in an hour or so and I hope you'll come see me there. Anything you have to tell me'll be held in strictest confidence, I guarantee you. By the way, my name's Jake Hatch and I work out of Omaha. That's not too hard to remember, is it? Okay, then, sorry you're all having to put up with this inconvenience."

Between cars, I asked Billy if he'd seen a twitch. He said he'd seen twitches, frowns, shifty eyes, pale faces, and he couldn't remember what all. So had I.

*So what the hell did that mean?*

It took me an hour to do the coaches, ten minutes apiece.

I didn't talk to anybody in the sleepers. If the emergency had been pulled in one of them, nobody was saying.

There was a party starting up in the lounge car. I don't know why Halt allowed the bar to open, but he did, and there are always people ready to party no matter what the hour. Nobody there'd seen a thing.

I picked the Amtrak people off one by one as they served coffee in the diner and the cars, but none of them had seen or heard anything strange. All had been asleep in the dormitory car except Sam Franklin, an old-timer who suffered sleeplessness and was in the diner adding to his insomnia with cups of coffee.

I sat down with him and Billy and had a cup of fresh brew.

"Nobody did nothing and nobody saw nothing," I

said. "So how, when, where, and why did the man fall off this train?" I took a menu and drew out the way the train was made up with Billy's help, starting from the back.

"Dormitory car, baggage car, two coaches, lounge, diner . . ."

"No, two coaches, lounge, sleeper, then the diner. Sleeper's got to be next to the diner, you know that," Billy said.

I made the correction. "That's right. So lounge, sleeper, diner, sleeper, the last two coaches, and the two engines."

"You forgot the deadhead right behind the second engine," Billy said.

We looked at one another.

When a car is deadheaded one place or another, riding empty on the front or back of a train so it can easily be separated without pulling the train apart, the doors aren't locked. There's usually just a little chain across the end doors saying that the car is not in use and is not to be entered except by railroad personnel.

When Billy and I made our way forward to the deadhead, we found it empty all right, but it hadn't always been empty that night. One of the side doors was open four or five inches, probably moving back and forth while the train was traveling and never slamming shut. The door on the other side looked shut but was off the latch as well.

The car had been cleaned in Chicago and there was no litter anywhere. Not a cigarette butt and not even a corn chip. But there was a briefcase lying on a seat. Not one of those fancy attaché cases, but an old-fashioned leather satchel with a flap and brass-buckled straps, something like a kid's bookbag.

There was nothing in it except a Denver newspaper.

"Had a ticket from Denver to Chicago and a Denver newspaper in the satchel," I mumbled to myself, "but goes falling off the train traveling the other way, from Chicago to Denver."

"That fella *fall* out of this car, you think?" Billy said.

"Or was pushed."

# Five

MORNING HAD GRAYED THE sky by the time Halt came looking for me an hour later. "I just heard back from the dispatcher in Denver. He had a hell of time reaching the coroner. The man's a farmer. Lives alone. Was out in the barn with a sick cow. Couldn't hear the telephone."

"Why didn't the dispatcher call the police?"

"I don't know, so don't ask me. Maybe because I told him to call the coroner. Henry Frye's a very literal sort of man. When Frye finally got him, the coroner said he was heading right out. Twenty minutes later he called back and said the bridge down the road didn't look safe enough to risk his truck on it."

"So he can't get here then?"

"Not until they can get a speeder over from the equipment shack down the road from Akron."

"I don't see how we can expect these passengers—"

28

"Hold your horses, Jake. I told dispatch to explain to the coroner what we found and the coroner told dispatch to tell me that if I could get another responsible party to sign a deposition that the fella's in two pieces he'd certify our victim dead."

"He's got that much confidence in us, has he?"

"Never mind the sarcastic remarks, Jake. Will you sign?"

"Well, of course I will. Let's pick up that poor bastard and get him into the baggage car."

We went out into the rain again. Bishop was still squatting beside the body as though he hadn't moved a muscle all this time. Billy went to the baggage car and told Jim Tiptree to open the doors.

I jumped up inside. Halt and Bishop lifted the body on the stretcher up to Billy and me. We put it down on some crates. Water dripped off the corpse and the tarps onto the planks.

"We'll mark the section of track here with flags," Halt said.

Billy gathered some up from a locker and handed them out.

When that was done, Halt and Bishop clambered aboard. We all started to leave the baggage car when Tiptree said, "You're not leaving that here unattended? A body can't travel in a baggage car unattended."

"All right," I said. "I'll sit with it into Akron."

They all filed out, leaving me sitting with the corpse.

After we got moving again, Tiptree said he was sorry but that was the rules. I said it was all right; I could handle it.

The train rocked along. Rounding a curve, the car swayed one way and then the other, slamming hard against the keepers when it hit the straightaway. Something fell out of the corpse's pocket and onto the floor with a small, dull sound.

I reached over and picked up a coin. I hadn't noticed it when I had the change in my hand. It looked like a plugged nickel. I tied it up in the corner of my handkerchief.

# Six

WHEN WE PULLED INTO Akron, more than three hours late, the rain had settled down to a steady drizzle that turned the sun into a pewter bowl that gave no warmth.

Halt, Billy, Laws, and me congregated on the platform while Fred Keely, the station agent, eyed us from the window of his office for a second, then came shambling out with this other fellow who was wearing a small-brimmed Stetson hat.

*I figured the coroner was about to declare our victim dead.*

Keely introduced us to Howard Freeman. He took off his glove and we shook hands all around like a bunch of Elks meeting at a convention.

"How's your cow?" I said.

"My what?"

"Dispatcher said you had a sick cow."

Color came and went in his face like he was a shy kid. "Oh, that. It's nothing much. Thanks for asking."

He was about as big as Bishop, with the same pale, open, honest face under his hat common in the farmlands of the Midwest. He wore wire-rimmed spectacles that kept misting up. He'd take out a blue bandanna and carefully clean them every so often. He smiled a lot.

"You've had your shock for the week, have you?" he said, putting his glove back on.

"It'll do me for the year," I said.

Halt handed over the deposition he'd written up and which we'd both signed.

"I don't know what use this is," Freeman said, "but I've learned that it's smart to always have something to cover your ass. Maybe I should go down and have a look now."

We broke up into pairs on the way to the baggage car. Me and Freeman, Halt and Keely, with Billy and Laws bringing up the rear.

"You been coroner long?" I asked.

"Not too long. I didn't go after it. Some people ran me for the office when I wasn't looking. I slaughter my own livestock, so I guess folks figured there was nothing I'd see in the job would bother me. We get our share of messy accidents around here on the farms." He looked at me like a one-eyed sparrow, peering down at me from above the misted lenses of his spectacles. "I know you?"

"I've spent some time around here."

"Have you?" he said, inviting further confidences, but not about to ask right out.

"I've got friends live outside of town," I said.

"Farmers?"

"He was until he got killed. She lives in the house but rents the acres."

"Threshing accident about four years ago?"

"That sounds about right."

"Carl Wister? You were a friend of Carl's?"

"Carl and Maggie's."

We reached the baggage car. Freeman put his hands on the floor, heaved himself up, and tucked his feet under him like an acrobat. I scrambled aboard as best I could, getting a splinter in my hand for trying to match him.

We hunkered down by the corpse and I pulled the tarpaulin aside.

"Yes, I'd say that fella's dead," Freeman said. "Cover the poor bastard back up."

Five minutes later we were standing around on the platform again, right-footing left-footing it, trying to figure out what came next. A few of the town's early birds had gathered in the magical way they'll do wherever there's some sensation or tragedy. They weren't pushy; nobody had to tell them to stand back. They just stood there wide-eyed, chewing their cuds.

"All I'm here for is to declare somebody dead, conduct the inquest, and call for an investigation if I think it's warranted," Freeman said.

"When will you have the hearing?" I asked.

"Any day soon. This looks like an easy one."

"What'll you do with the body meanwhile?"

"The medical examiner'll want to do an autopsy. They could send an ambulance from Denver, but as long as you've got the body already aboard the train, I don't see any reason why you can't just take it on into the city, do you?"

"I do," Halt spoke right up. "All bodies to be shipped by common carrier are to be embalmed—"

"If their condition permits," Freeman said.

"Otherwise hermetical sealing is required," Halt said. "There's also the matter of who's to authorize the shipment and who's to get billed for the drayage charges."

"I think maybe we should have taken the body to McCook," I said, half joking, half serious, but one hundred percent frustrated with Halt. "Nebraska law doesn't require embalming or sealing unless the deceased died of a communicable disease."

"I'd like to talk this over with the sheriff," Freeman said, hoping to get out of the web Halt was spinning before we were all hopelessly entangled. "I wonder where George McGilvray is anyway?"

"Maybe nobody thought to inform him," Laws said, with a sly glance at Halt Ennery.

"I reported the incident to the dispatcher according to regulations," Halt said in a huff, touchy as a hound with a sore paw. "What the fool did after that can't be laid at my door. One way or another, I'm moving this train inside of twenty minutes."

He peered at the sky as the sun broke through.

"Schedules ain't sacred, Halt," Laws said.

"They are to me," Halt snapped back, his temper frayed right down to a nub.

"You're the one who's holding up the parade."

"Why don't we just off-load the body and let Keely sign for it as though it were unconsigned freight?" I asked, trying to give Halt his out and everybody else a chance to go about their business.

"Can I do that?" Keely said.

"Of course you can do it."

"How do I route the paperwork?"

"Back to the front office. They'll tell you what to do."

"What the hell would the railroad have to do with deciding what's to be done with a corpse?"

"Not a damn thing. But by the time they get around to saying so, Sheriff McGilvray'll show up and take responsibility. That way there'll be no chance of you or me or anybody from the railroad getting hit with any flying debris."

"You know something about covering ass too," Freeman said.

"Where's that body going to be kept in the meantime?" Laws said, unable to keep from putting in his two cents. "You going to shove it into the cold-drink machine? I say we should carry it to Denver and turn it over to the medical examiner there. They'll thank us for it."

"Well, it's really not up to you, is it, Laws?" Halt said.

"Well, here's what we'll do," I said. "I'll stay on here with the body as the official representative of Burlington Northern until we get McGilvray or some other properly constituted authority to take official possession of the body. You go on ahead. All I ask you to do is write down what you saw, if anything, last night—"

"This morning," Halt said, a stickler for accuracy as well as for running things on time.

35

"—and ask everybody on the Burlington Northern crew to do the same."

"What's that supposed to prove?" Laws said.

"I haven't got a clue," I said. "How am I supposed to know what anybody saw or didn't see, heard or didn't hear? Maybe something one person writes down won't check with something somebody else writes down. Maybe something somebody writes down *will* check with something somebody else writes down. Why do I have to explain every damn little thing to you, Laws?"

"Well, you don't. I was only asking."

"So all right. Is what I'm asking for okay with everybody?"

"Okay, not okay, it's the only sensible thing to do," Billy said, closing off any more discussion.

"You want to get a wagon, Laws, and get that bundle out of the baggage car?" Halt said.

"I notice nobody's gone looking for the sheriff yet," Laws said, getting in his last shot.

"No reason to," Keely said. "Here he comes now."

A tall, lean drink of water was crossing the street from the Donut Shop across from the station, taking his time, carefully looking up and down the street, though there wasn't a vehicle in sight. He was carrying a big camp Thermos by its handle.

A blond, curly-headed woman, in a pink waitress's uniform with a white apron and a sweater thrown around her shoulders, trotted just a pace or two behind him. She had a cardboard carton in her hands.

I've known George McGilvray for some time now. Small as Washington County is, George's no hicktown sheriff leaning against a wall growing a belly. He'd been a precinct captain in Denver until he retired out to Akron and had been appointed to the sheriff's job, with some reluctance, only after old man Chickering dropped dead of a heart seizure. He'd run unopposed ever since and would probably die in office too.

He was a very friendly man, but somewhere along the line he'd taken on the habit of scarcely ever smiling when he was on duty. His long Scots face, pale blue eyes, and gray hair cut short gave him the look of some old-time Presbyterian minister, ready to comfort you one minute and smack you for cause the next.

"Having a railroad convention?" he asked when he joined the crowd. "Hello, Freeman, long time no see. And how are you doing, Jake?"

"Hangin' in. How's Bess?" I asked, sticking out my hand.

"Oh, she's good," he said.

*I knew she probably wasn't. His wife had arthritis very bad, but he wasn't the sort to air his troubles.*

"How come nobody thought to tell me you had a dead man on the train?" he said, very soft and mild-mannered.

I knew he was irked.

"Well, the fact is," Halt said, "I left it up to the dispatcher in Denver to do what he was supposed to do according to the book."

"Not everybody's read the book," George said, looking at Laws as he trundled the handcart with the tarp-covered body parts on it up to where we stood. The briefcase was on the corpse's chest.

"Lucky for me old Chuck Keppler was on the train and came across the street to spread the news," George went on.

He bent down with the ease of a much younger man and picked up the briefcase. "Anything important in this?"

"Just a Denver newspaper," I said.

"On a train that hadn't pulled in there yet." He laid it aside, then flicked back the top of the tarp.

"Doesn't happen to be somebody from around here, does it?" I asked.

"Don't know him. Looks like he's been bled white."

I lifted up the side of the tarp so he could see it all.

"I've seen a lot, but that's the first time I've ever seen that," he said. "Small feet," he added, pointing to the wet slip-ons.

We dropped the tarp. George tucked it in all around, like he was a nurse making a patient comfortable, then stood up.

The waitress was passing out coffee in Styrofoam cups in the shelter of the wall, far enough away so she didn't have to look at the horrible mess everybody else was trying to get a look at. The carton was on the bench and I could see it was filled with sweet rolls. She wasn't being a sister of mercy; she was collecting from the gallery for everything they took. She saw me looking and lifted her eyebrows and an empty cup. I counted heads and raised ten fingers twice, saying that I was buying coffee and sweet rolls for the bunch of us.

"This is about the damnedest accident I've ever seen," George said.

"Maybe it's not an accident," I said.

"What makes you say that?" Freeman said.

"There's nothing on the body to say who this fella is."

"You looked?"

"I went through his pockets and put it all back except this." I handed the little book to George. "I was trying to find out who he was in case he was traveling with somebody on the train and they hadn't missed him yet."

"So?" George said.

"So, he had no wallet."

"You think it was robbery?"

"That's what I'd say, except he's got money in a clip in the pocket of his trousers. It looks like he met somebody in a deadhead the train was hauling. But if that means anything, I don't know what."

The waitress came over with the ten coffees, some packets of sugar, sweetener, and powdered whitener. Those who wanted, took. I noticed that the waitress handed Freeman his coffee and knew him well enough not to have to ask him if he liked it any other way but black. He thanked her and called her Millie.

"Maybe we should get him under cover and have another look through his pockets," Freeman said.

I remembered the nickel and started to reach for it.

"I don't think so," George said. "I'd just as soon wait until we get the medical examiner in from Denver."

Freeman flushed, then turned pale the way he had before. His face was a barometer of his feelings. His eyes flicked to Millie. I could see he didn't like being challenged in front of her. But he didn't sound angry when he smiled and said, "Well, Sheriff, I'm the coroner, duly elected, and I could order the body searched and take the contents of his pockets in charge."

George just stared at the bigger man. "I don't see any sense in chewing our cabbage twice."

Freeman didn't stop smiling when he said, "We'll chew it if I say we'll chew it. I'll just go get a manila envelope from Keely and we'll have a look."

The blonde turned away and went back to get the sweet rolls.

"Upstart," George said, staring at the back of the departing Freeman.

"I had the idea that Freeman has been around here longer than you have," I remarked.

"Oh, no. He's only been around a couple of years. Maybe less."

"You don't like him much?"

George turned his ice-blue eyes to me and tapped his nose.

I knew what he was saying. There are times a cop can tell that there's something wrong about somebody but can't say exactly what. It's what cops call growing a nose and every cop grows one or has no success to speak of. Some noses are better for some things than other things. The one I've grown can smell out a thief or a pickpocket in a convention of saints.

Freeman came back with one of those nine-by-twelve routing envelopes with the string closure just about the time that Millie, carefully not looking at the body, came back with the pastries.

"I don't think so, thank you very much, Millie,"

George said, taking a pair of rubber surgical gloves out of his jacket pocket. Smart big-city cops always carry around a pair because they never know what they'll be asked to stick their hands into. George had never given up the habit.

"Are they all jelly doughnuts?" I asked, peering into the carton.

"I'm sorry. That's all that's left," Millie said.

"Then I think I'll do without."

It didn't bother the trainmen. They all took one. Laws took two. Then they got on the train. They were waving to me and grinning as I got my cash out of my pocket and found a twenty in the middle.

"Hey, no," Freeman said. "We can't let you go standing treat, a stranger in town and all."

"I'd give you the coffee and buns for free except Calvin wouldn't like it," Millie interjected.

"Calvin?"

"My husband."

"Put your money away, Mr. Hatch," Freeman insisted. "I'll settle up with Millie later."

She flashed him an up-and-sideways glance and a little smile curled her lips for a second as though she'd seen the double meaning in his offer even if he hadn't meant it. Freeman colored again. Millie trotted off, pulling the sweater around her shoulders.

"You wanted to be in on this," George said.

The three of us knelt around the body and went through the same routine I'd gone through on my own beside the tracks. Only this time George named off each item as Freeman wrote it down on the envelope and I dumped them in.

Freeman was a very thorough man, examining the cigarette butts as though they could talk, fingering every penny, nickel, dime, and quarter as though they could too.

I still held back the nickel tied in my handkerchief because I figured if George had the instinct not to trust Freeman, I wouldn't trust him either.

Finally we stood up.

"I think I'm going to call the state police," George said. "If this turns out to be robbery with violence, I'd just as soon somebody took it over. We're not equipped."

"Now, wait a second, George," I said. "No sense calling in a crowd until we at least hear what the medical examiner has to say."

"I think it's actually pretty cut and dried," Freeman said. "The verdict's going to be death by misadventure."

George didn't take kindly to being told how to think, though Freeman was grinning all over his face as if to say we were all friends speaking our minds and no offense intended.

"This is eating into your day, isn't it, Howard?" George said, flat-voiced and flat-eyed, taking the envelope from his hand.

For a minute it looked like Freeman was going to assert his coroner's rights over the property, but he decided he'd gone far enough in challenging George. He smiled and said, "Well, I don't get called on to earn my pay as coroner very often."

"But I guess you've done all you can do right at the moment."

"I guess I have. Sheriff, I want to apologize for the

way I talked to you just now. I'll just have to blame lack of sleep."

George nodded, but didn't break out any smiles in return. We put the body in a tool locker and Freeman took off in his pickup.

George and I walked over to his office, which was just down the block, so he could call the medical examiner's office in Denver. It was nine o'clock in the morning and I was getting hungry.

"What time is the M.E. apt to get here?"

"Well, it's a hundred-and-ten-mile drive from Denver. I'd give him an hour to get started and two and a half hours on the road. Four hours on the outside, let's say. So, after I make the call, you can come home with me and get some breakfast."

*I figured breakfast with Janel over to Fort Morgan, thirty-five miles away, was already a lost cause, but Maggie Wister lived on a farmstead about three miles outside of Akron. If I could borrow a bicycle from Keely, the station master . . .*

I tapped my forehead with my finger, acting like I was thinking about big errands I could take care of as long as I was there in Akron. "I thought I might borrow Keely's bicycle and maybe—"

"Take a pedal down the county road along the way to Platner?"

"Well, uh," I said.

"Maybe have a visit with the Widow Wister?"

"What makes you say that?"

"There's not much happens around here I don't hear about."

We stopped outside his office door.

He offered to drive me over to Maggie's, but the

rain had stopped altogether, the sun was yellow and warm, the air old-fashioned and sweet, and Keely was glad to lend me his bicycle.

When I got to Maggie's, I went around the back to see if she was in the kitchen. She wasn't, so I went to the front and pushed the bell. No bell rang because Maggie was deaf. The push button made a light blink in every room in the house. In a minute or so the door opened and she was standing there smiling at me.

She welcomed me with a kiss, letting me know that she was glad to see me again. Maggie keeps things separate and apart, one thing rarely slopping over into another. There's friendliness and there's passion. There's conversation and there's lovemaking.

While we shared some jam and butter on bread warm from the oven, I told her about the horrible experience I'd lived through in the small hours of the morning, she reading my lips, gazing at my mouth with a soft intensity that always seems more than a little erotic to me. I told her I was sleepy.

# Seven

I JUST BARELY MADE it back to the station before the M.E. arrived from Denver in a morgue ambulance. His name was Walter Bosley, a little fussy fellow who reminded me right off the bat of a banty rooster looking for someone to put his spurs to.

"What's going on, asking an examiner to drive a hundred miles to do a body? Ties up a vehicle and a driver for a whole day, not to mention my time. You should've shipped the corpse to me. How come the office didn't tell you that?"

George reared back. I was afraid that Bosley was about to get a piece of his mind. Ordinarily I let people have at it, but this time I stepped right in.

"Well, Mr. Bosley," I said, "there's this question of jurisdiction."

"Shouldn't be any problem about jurisdiction. Proper procedure would've been to call the State

Board of Health in Denver. That office has precedence over any other in matters constituting a potential health hazard."

"Well, thank you for telling me that," I said. "You've just taught me something."

Bosley looked at me as though he sincerely doubted my expression of appreciation. "Where's the corpse?" he said.

When we took him out to the equipment shed, he looked down at the mound under the tarp. "I can't examine it down on my knees. I've got this back. Have you got any place we can get it up closer to my hands and eyes?"

We put it up on the wood box where Keely kept his fuel and kindling.

Bosley unwrapped the corpse. The ambulance driver, who'd probably seen it all, just stood there chewing on a toothpick.

"To tell you the truth," Bosley said, "I could've sent one of my assistants, but it's not every day a body turns up cut in half by a train. It's just a wonder what that kind of tremendous weight can do, isn't it?"

He took off his overcoat and his suit jacket, in spite of the cold, rolled up his sleeves, and put on a pair of surgical gloves. Then he started poking around. After a while he got a pair of scissors out of his bag and cut away some of the clothing.

"You want to look at the inventory of the things that were in his pockets?" George asked.

"I've got no interest in what he had in his pockets."

George stepped back and Bosley went at it. Of course, he was just doing a gross examination. The real autopsy would take place in the proper surroundings back in Denver.

Finally he put the tarpaulin back and stripped off his gloves.

"Is there anything there we haven't already seen?" I said.

"What do you think you've already seen?" Bosley replied.

"Well, a man who's been mashed and pulled apart under the wheels of a train."

"Then, you haven't seen much."

"How's that?"

"You haven't seen that the two halves don't match."

I don't know if my mouth fell open, because I couldn't see myself, but I know that George's did for the first time in living memory.

Bosley was enjoying himself. "The head, arms, and torso are those of a male. The legs and pelvis are those of a female."

"Little shoes," George said.

# Eight

YOU'D THINK GETTING TOGETHER a search party would
be an easy thing like it is in the movies. Well, it isn't.
First of all you don't want everybody and his brother
tramping around the countryside, maybe getting lost,
maybe breaking a leg, maybe getting themselves killed
in any one of twenty different ways. Even in places
where men are used to the difficulties of the terrain,
most of them have jobs and businesses and troubles
which make it hard for them to just drop tools and go
tramping off through the woods. Also, people will
come out to search in one case and not another. They
are a lot more apt to join in a search for a missing
child or some backpacking greenhorn than for an
experienced hunter or the local drunk. And they sure
as hell don't see the urgency in going out looking for
somebody already dead.

So it took nearly all of the next day, on toward dusk

and cold as hell, before George had collected the men and gear needed for a search along the railroad right of way.

*How long would it take for anyone to make up a search party to come looking for me if I should get myself killed or gone missing? Living alone the way I do, going off here and there for days, even weeks, at a time, who the hell would even know I wasn't where I was supposed to be? Certainly not Mrs. Dunleavy, my landlady back in Omaha. It was enough to make a man feel sorry for himself.*

When George came back to the station, he had a dozen men with him. At first I thought Freeman was walking alongside him, but then I saw it was a stout woman, wearing a blanket coat and a small-brimmed Stetson, who looked a lot like him, even down to the foggy specs.

Freeman was walking just behind her, but he speeded up and passed her when he spotted me.

"Sometimes, no matter how hard you try, you find your ass out there in the breeze, don't you?" he said, grinning. "Is our friend . . . I mean friends . . . still around? I'd like to have another look."

"Bosley took them back to Denver in the ambulance."

"The whole kit and caboodle?"

"What do you mean by that?"

"I mean is Denver taking over the case and are we just going out like errand boys to find the extra pieces?"

"I don't think there's any question about any glory in this."

"That's not exactly what I meant." He flushed and

found another start. "He find anything else on the bodies?"

"Like what?"

A frown popped up between his eyebrows. The high color paled like it was just washed out. "Did George give you his wild hair to stick up your ass?" he said, low and soft. "I'm the coroner around here and I just asked you if maybe the medical examiner found any other evidence of who those unfortunates might be."

"And I just asked you what sort of evidence you had in mind?" I said blandly. "I've got no quarrel with you and don't want any, Mr. Freeman."

"I didn't mean—"

"The M.E. didn't find anything else. You can be sure if he had we'd have no reason to hide it from you."

He shook his head and grinned again. "Please don't mind me. I've been a little touchy the last couple of days."

"The cow."

"What? Oh, yeah, the cow. First I'm called out to certify a body that's been cut in half. Now here I am volunteering to go tramping around in the mud and cold." He reached out and took the woman's arm and drew her over. "This is Dixie Hanniford, lives down the road from my place."

"My name's Jake Hatch."

Dixie stuck out a hand as big as a man's and we shook. "Pleased to meet you."

"Likewise."

George got up on a baggage wagon. "People," he said, not raising his voice any louder than he had to.

"We only got the one speeder. For those who don't know what a speeder is—"

"Give us a little credit, Lord's sake," Dixie said.

"—it's a little electric cart that runs on the tracks."

"I used to ride one of them what had the seesaw handles when I was a girl," Dixie said.

"All right, Dixie," George said. "We can't all get aboard the speeder at once, so I'm going to break us up into two parties. One party'll take a couple of four-wheel drives along the road as far as Wager's Crossing. That's two miles west of where the train was stopped. Coroner Freeman'll lead that party."

"Howard couldn't find his ass with his hand in the dark," Dixie said. She winked at me through her granny glasses as Freeman gave her an affectionate shove with his shoulder.

"So you'll hold his hand, Dixie," George said. "I'll take the other party with me on the speeder two miles the other side of where the train stopped. The railroad detective, Jake Hatch, over there, tells me the spot is marked with flags. First party will move east, second party west to the flags. We've got to search the slopes along the grade. What we're looking for is two body halves."

"Sheriff," somebody piped up, "we'll have a hell of a time trying to find anything on those muddy slopes in the dark. We're not half as many as we should be."

"I know that, Charlie. I'm just taking a wild shot until we can gather together a bigger crowd to go out in the daylight."

"Why don't we just wait until we got it, then?" Charlie said.

"Two reasons. One, I can't just stand around with my thumb up my . . ." He stopped and glanced at Dixie.

She laughed and said, "I just used the word, George."

"And plenty more, no doubt," he said, working the joke for the good that was in it. Loosening the men up. Pointing it out without pointing it out that the one woman among them was making wisecracks instead of complaining. "The other reason is I'm afraid some animals could be out on the hunt now that the rain has stopped and I'd just as soon we found the pieces before they do. Okay, Freeman, pick your crew, but leave Jake Hatch with me."

Before Freeman moved away from me I said, "How come George is sending you by the road? I thought the bridge wasn't safe."

"Didn't look safe last night while it was raining," Freeman said. "It's not raining now and the river's down."

I went to the tracks and hopped aboard the speeder.

The wind cut my face and hands as the speeder rattled along toward the place on the tracks marked by the flags.

"Would a train running over a body make a bump?" George said.

"Not so's you'd notice," I said.

"So, it could've run over these people a good ways back from where we're going and dragged the two pieces?"

"Could've; they were dragged the distance it took for the train to stop after the emergency was pulled, but they'd be a lot more battered than they are if they'd been dragged much farther."

"Any idea about who pulled the emergency?"

"I questioned the Amtrak employees and made an announcement to the passengers. I was saving the Burlington Northern personnel until I got to Denver, but then I got left behind. I expect, if they'd seen anyone pull the cord, they'd have come forward already."

"This's been a long watch for you," George said.

"I'm feeling okay."

"Got some sleep over to the Widow Wister's, did you?"

"Well, yes, I got some."

The flags went by, hanging as still as crepe in the windless night until the breeze of the speeder's passing lifted them up like handkerchiefs waving us goodbye.

In another several minutes we were stopped two miles away.

Everybody piled off, breaking up in two parts, moving up and down the slopes on either side of the rails, shining bright-beamed torches everywhere, making a landscape of moving shadows.

When we found another half of a body, it was about a mile and a half from where we started searching and half a mile from the flags. It had taken our party two hours to get that far.

Charlie Preacher, the fella who'd raised the practical questions, yelled out and lifted up his arms until all the flashlights were turned on him. He looked as white as a ghost in the harsh glare of so many torches, but he was as self-possessed as anyone could expect when we all gathered around.

There was a dark bundle at his feet.

"It's the other half of the man," Preacher said.

"The animals been at it?" George said.

"Now, how the hell would I know that, the condition that poor bastard's in?"

"Tracks," George replied.

"Oh." Preacher moved his light all around the body. "No, nothing's been at it."

We searched with extreme care all around the spot, both sides of the tracks, reckoning that if three pieces had been found that close together, the fourth piece might not be far away. But by the time the other search party joined up with us about three hours later, we'd had no more luck. The only thing we'd found was a soft felt hat, caught on a bush, which could have belonged to the dead man, and just as easy could've not.

The upper half of the woman was still missing.

We stood around listening to the swollen stream rushing along at the bottom of the southern slope.

"She could be down there," I said.

"Just what I was thinking," George said.

"This isn't the time to be wading around in running water," Dixie said.

It was getting on to midnight, so George decided to call it quits until the next morning. He put Freeman, Dixie, Keely, himself, me, Preacher, and another fella on the speeder with the half a body and left the rest to go tramping back the two miles to the vehicles waiting at Wager's Crossing.

# Nine

BACK AT THE STATION, Keely and the other man went home. Dixie, Freeman, and Preacher hung on while George and I went through the pockets. A set of keys, a handkerchief, thick with mucus.

"Must have had a hell of a cold," George said.

There was thready blood in it. "Busted a blood vessel blowing his nose too hard," I said. Some of the mess was on my fingers. George wiggled his rubber-gloved fingers, telling me I should take up better habits. I cleaned my fingers on my own handkerchief, feeling the nickel in the corner of it, still not willing to hand it to George with Freeman around.

George daintily dropped the last item into the manila envelope Freeman was marking. "Sticky little mess of half-melted roll candies. Still no billfold or wallet."

"So the woman had the money in the clip but this fella had nothing," I said.

"Or she had *his* money, like we said before," George said.

Freeman got up out of his squat. "Well, okay, that's that. I certify this fella's dead too. Anybody brings in any more pieces make up your minds for yourselves and don't call me till morning."

He walked off with Dixie.

"Funny fella," Preacher said, then went home too.

George and I wrapped the pelvis and legs in a tarp and stowed them in the equipment locker off to the side of the platform. I laid the hat on the knees. We hung around, waiting for the others, just to show them that we were the kind of leaders who wouldn't go to our own warm beds before the troops were sent to theirs.

When they came back, a few of them were loud and boisterous, having consulted a bottle somebody'd brought along to guard against the chill. George sent them all home with his thanks.

I said I'd be going over to the hotel but George invited me back to his place instead.

"You sure we won't disturb Bess?" I said.

"No, she'll probably still be awake. We'll just lock this property up first."

His offices weren't much. Just a bare-boards reception area with a counter. Nobody behind it. The switchboard had a red patch light on. In George's office there was just a desk, an old worn leather chair, a beat-up green file cabinet, a wooden chair, a wastebasket made of wire, and a fat safe. I stood there looking at a big topographical map of the area. It was the only decoration on the walls except for some framed citations. George pulled open the unlocked safe and put the envelope into a green metal box.

When we got to his place, a big, comfortable old house at the end of a tree-lined road, Bess greeted us with smiles.

She was in her flannel nightgown and robe, slippers on her feet and her long hair in a single braid down her back.

*I thought about how much trouble and pain doing that with her hair every night must cause her. Or did George usually braid it for her?*

She put her cheek to my cheek, her poor twisted, swollen hands resting on my shoulders for an instant.

"Come into the kitchen where it's warm," she said.

There was a cat curled up on a rag rug by the heavy cast-iron stove which was throwing out plenty of heat and holding back the night chill that filled the rest of the house. There was a pot of soup simmering at the back. Bess moved a big coffeepot onto a spot glowing red, wincing as she did so.

George winced too. He laid out two bowls without asking, took bread from the box and butter from the keeper, and brought over the soup pot. I ladled out the portions.

When the coffeepot started to steam, he was up and there to pour before Bess could get to it.

"I'm going to do without the coffee," I said. "I need my sleep."

Bess sat down with us, warming her hands around her coffee cup. "So, tell me."

We told her everything we knew.

"What do you make of it?" she said.

"Not very much, so far," I said. "We know that one of them was aboard with a ticket. We don't know about the other."

"Which one had the ticket?"

"The woman. She was using it for a bookmarker. Assuming it's her book. There was no ticket on the other person, but there was no wallet either. It could've been stolen. Or it could've fallen out along the tracks. The woman had a money clip in her pocket which could've belonged to the man, but we've got no way of knowing that for sure either."

"Was she wearing jeans or dungarees?"

"She was wearing slacks or the trousers to a suit. What makes you ask?"

"Women don't often carry money in their pockets. We just never got into the habit because we've always got a purse or a bag in our hands. Young woman?"

"I'd say so."

"If she was at all stylish, the slacks would be cut just right. So that would be another reason why she wouldn't be carrying money in her pockets. It would ruin the line."

"I'd say the money in the clip could've been the man's money," George said.

"Anybody think to count it?" I asked.

"I didn't, did you?" George said.

"We're not much when it comes to being detectives, are we?" I said, disgusted with myself.

"What are you two on about?" Bess said.

"Well, depending on the amount of money in the clip, we could make a fair guess about whether the woman stole the money from the man or if he'd turned it over to her," I said.

"How could you do that?"

"If it was a payoff of some kind, it would be a fairly big amount and would probably count out to the nearest hundred."

"I'd never think of that," Bess said, with a touch of admiration in her voice.

Feeling better for the praise, I said, "George would've, sooner or later."

"What sort of a book was it?" Bess asked.

"Poems."

"You wouldn't happen to remember what sort of poems."

*Collected Sonnets.*

"A small book?"

"Very small; smaller than a paperback. Just a little thing about so big."

"Hard cover or soft?"

"Hard," I said, wondering at the way a woman's mind worked.

"A little present from a man, I'd bet," Bess said.

"The lipstick on the handkerchief in her pocket," I said. "He could've got some on him if they kissed and she could've wiped it off with his handkerchief, then put it in her own pocket."

George reached across the table and touched his wife's hand and said, "It's getting late. Jake's about to fall face-first into what's left of his soup." He looked at me. "How long's it been since you saw a bed? Not mentioning the Widow Wister's?"

"The Widow Wister?" Bess exclaimed. "Whoever says that anymore?"

"Well," I said, "I've been up, except for a short nap at Maggie's, since seven o'clock in the morning day before yesterday. Thanks for the offer, but I think I'll sleep on the train."

"Train doesn't leave for Omaha until eleven to-night."

"I'm not going home, I'm going to Denver. That train leaves five minutes before five this morning."

"What're you going to Denver for?"

"I thought I might take the rest of the man with me. I'd like to be there when Bosley finishes the autopsy on him."

"Well, if you're sure you want to be such an eager beaver."

"Thing like this, the sooner you get to it the better."

"Eager beaver," Bess said.

"What's that?" George said.

"Nobody's said that for years, either."

Her saying things like that made me feel a little old. I thought of Janel Butterfield's wonderful country breakfasts and Charlotte Shumway's cottage garden over to McCook in Nebraska and Maggie Wister's lovely feather bed not half a dozen miles away. For a minute there I was ready to change my mind and go toddling off to bed in the McGilvray guest room but George sighed, stood up, and went to get his coat off the hook.

"Where you going?" I said.

"Help you get the body aboard."

"I can do that with the baggageman. You don't have to go out again."

"You might as well take the personal property along with you. If we're going by the book, that stuff should stay with the bodies."

"I notice you don't lock your safe—"

"Nothing in it to steal."

"—so why can't you just give me an extra key, and when I'm through, I'll leave it on the desk. The Yale lock'll latch itself."

"I've got a radio transmitter in the other room. I'll call the deputy in the cruiser and tell him not to shoot you if he sees you in the office." He stood there with one arm in the sleeve of his coat. "On the other hand, maybe it would be just as easy if I drove you on down."

"It's six blocks," I said. "The walk'll fool my body into believing it's had a good night's sleep."

"For heaven's sake, you two," Bess said. "Alphonse and Gaston. Who's going to be the most polite. Hush up, George, give Jake the extra key and thank God for considerate friends."

I was glad she'd spoken up. We could have gone around the mulberry bush for days. "Why don't you two go on up to bed? I'll let myself out when it's time for me to be going."

Bess smiled her thanks at me behind George's back. She was as concerned about his health and welfare as he was about hers.

They went off to bed. I sat there remembering the first line of the poem on the page marked by the railroad ticket.

"How do I love thee, let me count the ways."

Then I thought about the three cigarette butts in the man's pocket. It was a soldier's habit.

# Ten

I ALMOST NODDED OFF sitting there by the warm stove. My chin touched my chest and I jerked my head up quick. I sat there listening to the night sounds of the house, all the creaking, clicking, and sighing.

*There's a different voice to a house with more than one person living in it than a house with nobody in it but yourself.*

I got out of there and on my way before I started feeling really sorry for myself.

After a rain like the one we'd had, the temperature usually cranks up a notch or two, but it was almost balmy outdoors.

The streets were quiet except for an orange cat who walked half a block with me, glancing up once as if to say that only nightbirds like him and me understood the beauty of the dark and the quiet.

When I passed the Donut Shop, I was surprised to see some lights on. Somebody wearing a coat and a knitted hat was moving around inside. I went up close to the front door and peered in. The person whirled around, sensing an intruder. I could see it was Millie, looking morning-pinched around the eyes and mouth. She grinned and pulled off her cap, her bleached blond hair spilling out as she walked over and unlatched the door.

"We're not open yet," she said. "I haven't even got the coffee going." I looked over her shoulder at the big brushed steel urn with the glass capacity measures on the side in which they brewed their coffee instead of in those glass pots for making it a pot at a time that most restaurants use nowadays. "I could boil a pot of water quick and make you a cup of instant." She made a face. "I know. Instant's not much, but I keep it around for myself. I've got to have something to open my eyes at this ungodly hour while I'm waiting for the real stuff to cook up."

"Thanks," I said, "but I'm on my way out of town and I've got a few things to do before the train pulls in. I'm surprised anybody's here at all this early in the morning."

"Well, we open at six and it takes more than an hour these days to get everything warm and perking. I take mornings sometimes. Calvin hates getting up in the dark. So, will you be coming back?"

"I expect I will."

"I'll be seeing you, then," she said, and shut the door.

I went on over to the sheriff's office in the storefront

a block away from the railroad station and the Donut Shop. The key slipped into the lock like a knife into butter.

Inside, there was a light on over the counter and the red patch light glowed on the switchboard. The door to George's office was opened a crack and there was a light on in there too. I thought that it was a funny sort of light as I walked across the room and put my hand out to shove the door open all the way.

The funny light was a bull's-eye lantern sitting on the floor facing the safe. There was somebody crouched down in front of it. George's desk blocked most of my view. All I could see was hat and the impression of eyeglasses flashing dully in the light of the lantern as whoever it was turned around when he felt the draft from the open door.

"Hey," I said, thinking it might be the duty officer and about to tell him I was Hatch and did George get him on the radio to tell him I was coming down to pick up the property envelopes. All I got out was the first word because the lantern was picked up and swung at my head as somebody big and bulky tried to go right through me on the way to the door.

I ducked but managed to get hold of a piece of a mackinaw, enough to send the intruder sprawling but not enough to hold on to, as I went down. The light of the lantern went out. We both scrambled to our feet at the same time. I started moving forward when something flashed out of the big shadow which was all I could see in front of the door to the outer office. There was a crack like a tree limb snapping off on a bitter cold night and I felt a sting on the side of my face that knocked me sideways.

The shadow was gone. I heard heavy footsteps running through the front office and the outer door slamming. I put one hand to my ear. It was warm and wet. I reached out for the light switch.

A car pulled up outside, its wheels spraying gravel.

"Hey, you!" I heard somebody shout. "Hey, you! Stop in the name of the law!"

*That was a nice old-fashioned touch.*

The safe door was wide open. The metal box was on the floor and open too. But the manila property envelopes were still there. A deputy, bundled up in an anorak, gloves, and a hat with ear flaps, stood in the doorway.

"You must be Jake Hatch." He walked up to me and gently pulled my hand away from my ear. "Somebody clipped off your earlobe," he said in a voice that showed interest but very little concern. "I'd better call the sheriff."

George arrived at the office ten minutes after the deputy, Dan Crack, who'd scarcely said another word since telling me I'd lost a piece of ear, gave him the call.

*So, he'd had to go out before sunrise after all.*

"Sorry we had to get you out of bed," I said. "After all my good intentions."

"Dan?" George said.

"Sheriff," Crack said.

"Now that I'm here, you want to go take a cruise around? Not the whole tour, just around the middle of town."

After Crack left, George looked at me again. "Clipped your ear," he said.

"I know that, George."

"It looks like it's stopped bleeding but I think you ought to have it looked at by Doc Crowder."

"I would do that except I'm catching the train to Denver in about fifteen minutes, so it'll just have to wait until I get to the morgue."

"That's all right, then. Maybe Bosley'll put a plaster on it for you. Now, what the hell you think this is all about?"

"Your guess is as good as mine," I said, wondering why people do like we do, saying the same things in the same way over and over again.

*Probably makes out-of-the-ordinary things seem ordinary. Probably makes us feel in charge when we know that things are spinning out of control.*

"Whoever it was, was going through the safe."

His eyes went to the metal box and the envelopes in it. "Didn't get anything?"

"Pick up the first envelope we sealed," I said.

George picked it up and said, "Yeah?"

"Jiggle it."

He stared at me and did what I asked him to do as though he were humoring a child. "So, all right, I jiggled it."

"Notice anything?"

He jiggled it again, then laid it down flat on the desk and checked the flap and the little hasp.

"They're intact," I said. "Take a look along the bottom."

He checked the bottom flap to see if somebody had made it come unstuck.

"Right here," I said, stepping over to show him the razor cut about an inch and a half long right along the fold. "Nobody'd ever notice it unless they knew there was supposed to be a small handful of change in there. The cut's just wide enough to let the coins slip through."

"Somebody broke into a sheriff's office, a safe, and a strongbox just to steal a couple of dollars in change?" George said.

"Well, the safe wasn't locked and the strongbox wasn't very strong," I reminded him. "The fact is whoever broke in didn't think they were taking much of a chance. Even so, somebody took a shot at me over something that's not worth a plugged nickel."

*Plugged nickel.*

I took out my handkerchief and unknotted the corner, letting loose the coin I'd put there for safe-keeping.

When I handed it to him, George looked it over.

"What's this?"

"A plugged nickel."

"It's not holed through," George said, being accurate.

"When I say plugged, I don't mean holed through. It just looks plugged."

"These marks look like they were stamped there with steel dies."

"That's my thought exactly."

"There's three marks. You know what they mean?"

"I haven't got a clue."

"Where'd you get it?"

"It fell out of one of the pockets belonging to one of the corpses while I was riding with their separate parts in the baggage car. I had no way of knowing which part it fell out of, even if I'd known there were two parts of two different people."

"Why didn't you hand this in before?"

"I was going to. Then Freeman almost had a fight with you over going through the pockets with him there. I figured if you didn't trust the man, I didn't trust the man."

"I never said I didn't trust him. I don't much *like* him, but I never said I didn't trust him."

"Well, I'm saying it, then."

The train whistle sounded a warning a mile down the track right where the highway cuts across it.

"How come you didn't show this to me while we were having our soup after we got home?"

"Well, how the hell do I know, George? I'm tired as hell and I was sleepy and we were talking about this and that and—"

"No need to get upset, Jake."

"Well, I mean, for God's sake, why do you ask me questions I can't answer first thing in the morning?"

"It's pretty lucky," George said.

"What's pretty lucky?"

"It's pretty lucky you're as sloppy and disorganized as me. Otherwise this nickel would've been in the property envelope where it belonged and the thief would've got it along with the rest."

"You think this is what he was looking for?"

"What do you think?"

I shrugged. "We got time to count that money," I said.

"Go ahead."

I slit open the bottom of the envelope a little more with my knife. I slid the money clip out into my hand. It was a plain silver clip, no initials, no engraving. Just the sterling mark stamped into the back of it.

The fold of bills was pretty thick. The top ten bills were hundreds. Under that were three singles, a five and a ten spot.

"Well, what do you make of that?" I said.

"Make of what?" George replied, watching me fan the money out.

I pointed to the way the bills were lined up, hundreds on top. "That's not the way a person keeps folding money, the big bills on top."

"How do they keep it?"

"You use a money clip?"

George pulled it out of his pocket.

"So, take a look at how you keep your money in it."

He pulled off the clip and unfolded his little packet of bills. "Ones on top and so on down the line."

"Practically everybody I know who uses a clip lays it out that way so when you pay for your groceries or hardware you have the smaller bills closest to hand. Mix them all up and you could have your attention elsewhere and end up dropping a twenty when you meant to drop a one. Have the big bills on top and you've got a gambler's flash roll which could invite a mugging."

"So, we got the clip from the woman's trousers. If the thousand was a payoff of some kind, she could've just folded them on top and stuck the whole thing back in her pocket."

"Or the man could've been the one paid off."

"How'd it get into her pocket?"

"Maybe she picked it."

"One minute you've got them kissing each other and the next minute you've got her picking his pocket," George complained.

"The two things aren't logistically incompatible," I said.

"I'll forget you said that," George said. This kind of speculation wasn't the kind of police work he was used to. "We're never going to find out what's what by saying what about this and what about that."

"Well, it doesn't hurt to try and figure out where the old trout is hiding before you go fishing," I said.

The Zephyr heading west pulled into the station across the street. I taped up the envelope and we hurried over to the platform, put the tarp-wrapped bottom of the man onto a luggage cart, and rolled it over to the baggage car. Jim Tiptree was dropping bundles of newspapers onto a wagon.

"What have you got there, another dead body?" he joked.

"That's exactly what we've got," I said.

He saw I was telling the truth. "Oh, for the good Lord's sake."

George and I lifted the bundle up and Tiptree dragged it a foot or so inside the door. "A body can't—"

"I'm coming along with it," I said, before he could give me the entire speech.

"Might have expected it," Tiptree said.

"How's that?"

"Well, it's right there in the paper."

The front page on the top bundle said TWO CUT IN HALF BY TRAIN. ONLY TWO HALVES FOUND.

"That should do it," I said. "That should get some other agencies nosing around."

"It's still our case until we're told different," George said.

"You decided you want it too?"

"Well, I can't have you running around with your ass hanging out in the cold wind all by yourself, Jake."

Down the platform a way, Halt Ennery yelled, "All aboard," and stood there looking at me as though daring me to hold up his train one more time.

"You want somebody to go along with you?" George asked.

"What for?"

"Well, for company. Somebody to talk to on the way."

"Who did you have in mind?"

"I could spare my deputy, Dan Crack."

"No, thanks. I'll get more chat out of those legs than I ever would out of old Dan."

We were making gruesome jokes again, standing alongside the bottom half of a body, me fiddling with what could have been the man's hat. All of a sudden, I remembered what a lot of men did with train tickets. They stuck them in their hatbands. Sure enough, there it was, a ticket from Chicago to Denver and back again.

"Well, that clears up one little mystery," George said.

"But still leaves us with the other. The man was going east to west from Chicago. The woman had a ticket for a trip west to east. What was she doing on a train going the wrong way?"

"And how did she get there?"

"And how did she get there?" I echoed.

"We'll have time to think about it when you get back. It's nothing that can't wait."

I agreed that gathering up the rest of the pieces and

getting the lower half of the man to Bosley in Denver took first consideration.

George stuck out his hand. "Come back when you can. If it's soon, you'll probably find me out on that goddamn mountainside."

Halt hollered, "All aboard!" again, so I scrambled into the baggage car, remembering the neat way Freeman had managed it the day before.

# Eleven

TIPTREE HAD THE DOOR to the baggage car opened more than a crack and was standing there looking out, swaying softly with the switch and sway of the baggage car.

"Indian summer," he said.

"Feels like it."

"You see the size of the moon tonight? Harvest moon. It was hanging up there like a Chinese lantern."

*The lyrics to an old song my mother used to sing came into my head. "Shine on, shine on harvest moon up in the sky. I ain't had no lovin' since January, February, June or July." It made me feel all melancholy, like a homeless child who'd grown sick and tired of the open road.*

I got up and stood beside him at the door.

73

"I didn't know you were given to poetic images, Jim," I said.

"I don't know about poetic, but you do get into your thoughts riding alone so much the way I do. Almost makes you see things."

He wanted to tell me something, but was hoping I'd worm it out of him for some reason.

"What sort of things?" I said.

"Well, like the things you think you see in that funny kind of violet-gray light that comes at false dawn."

"Any special things?"

"Like right there at the spot along the tracks where the bodies were found yesterday?" He stuck his head out the door a little, as if he could actually see the spot, then popped back in, his hair all tossed around his face, grinning like a kid from the exhilaration it gave him. "I was hanging out like that, trying to see if the flags Halt planted on the roadbed were still standing up?"

"Were they?"

"A couple. So, I was standing with my head out like that. As we got near the flags I saw something in the light. At first I thought it was a mountain cat or a bear."

"But it wasn't a mountain cat or a bear?"

"Well, I don't really know. I don't think so."

"Think about it."

"Whatever it was—whoever it was—turned away and hunched over as the train went past. There was something on it that flashed."

"Like metal?"

"Exactly."

"You get an impression of what it was?"

He stuck his head out the door a little bit, not as far as he'd done before, pretending to be following something along the road as it sped by, whipping his head from one side to the other, then pulled himself back inside again.

"Like that. It was that fast, so I can't be sure what I saw."

"Maybe a broken bottle shining out of the weeds?"

He seemed doubtful. "I think I saw a face and maybe the reflection off somebody's eyeglasses and this metal thing in their hands," he said, more certain, now that I challenged his experience, that it was something a lot stranger and more important than some animal and a broken bottle.

"What the hell would anybody be doing out along there in the dark?" I said.

"Another search party?"

"No. McGilvray's still looking for the missing half of the woman, but he'll be doing it in the daylight now that the only place left to search is down along that river."

"Well, I saw something," Tiptree said in a sturdy way as though daring me to call him a liar.

"I've no doubt," I said, wishing I'd had a glimpse of what he'd seen or thought he'd seen. "I want to stretch my legs. Is that okay?"

"Well, according to regulations . . ."

"Give me a little room here, for Pete's sake, Jim. No railroad inspector is suddenly going to appear out of the blue. . . ."

"All right. All right. I'm just saying, anything happens to that person you got laying there, ain't my fault."

"I'd swear to that," I said, and went out looking for Halt.

I found him in the dormitory car having a cup of coffee, hat and jacket off, conductor's purse sitting on the seat beside him.

"How's it going, Halt?" I said.

"I think we've got some of the curious aboard."

"You mean sightseers?"

"I mean people who stand around car wrecks."

"You telling me there's people would pay a fare to ride a train just because a couple of people fell off and got themselves killed?"

He looked at me as though he wasn't sure but that I was pulling his leg. "Of course there are. Where've you been all your life?"

I sat across from him and unbuttoned my jacket.

"Indian summer," he said.

"You see the size of the moon tonight?"

"I was holding puddles of it in my lap," he said, and smiled, looking young just like Tiptree had done.

"Did your crew do like I asked and write down their impressions of what happened the other night, Halt?"

He fumbled in the big leather purse on the seat beside him and came up with a legal-sized brown envelope. "The depositions are all in here."

"They're not depositions. Just statements. You read them?" I said, holding the envelope in my hands.

"Were they private?" he snapped.

"No. I just asked you did you read them?"

"Yes, I read them."

"Well, what did they say?"

"Not much of anything. What did you expect them to say? Just a waste of time, like I told you the other morning."

"You didn't tell me anything."

"Well, that's what I was thinking," he said. "When the emergency was pulled and we scrambled off the train, I knew what you knew and that was all there was to know. Charlie Tichenor was on the throttle and Billy Turk in the cab. They saw nothing but the track ahead. Laws Ruskel was reading a book. Harry Bishop was sleeping in the dormitory car with the Amtrak crew. He would've slept through the whole thing except one of the Amtrak stewards woke Harry up after he was woke up himself when the brakes slammed on. What the hell you staring at?"

"Just thinking."

"Well, if you're going to go on playing detective, you'd better get your nose to the ground and stop wasting my crew's time writing out useless stories."

"Why are you talking so goddamn mean to me?"

Halt brushed a hand across his face and rumpled his hair. "Don't ask me. I just got a feeling."

"What kind of feeling?"

"Just this funny feeling."

"For God's sake, Halt, you've got to talk plainer than that."

"The feeling this train isn't quits with this whole business yet."

"What makes you say that?"

"I was sitting here drinking this coffee and looking out the window when we passed the place where we dragged those pieces out from under the train." He

77

stopped and cut his eyes left and right like a skitterish horse.

"Yeah?" I said, urging him to finish whatever it was he was trying to say.

"I saw something."

"Something?"

"Somebody. Somebody waving a . . ."

"Waving what, Halt?"

"It looked like some kind of funny cross, shining in the dark."

"I don't think so, Halt. I don't think you had a religious experience. I don't think you saw a ghost or a spirit. I think you saw what Jim Tiptree saw."

"He saw something too? What'd he see?" Halt said, leaning forward eagerly as though I were about to tell him something that would get him off the hook.

"Probably a bear walking the mountain and a reflection off some broken glass."

Halt collapsed back into his seat. After a minute he said, "That's not what I saw." But he didn't say anything more.

I sat there and read the individual accounts of what the Burlington Northern crew remembered about that night. There was nothing in them worth a thing to me. After riding in silence for a while, I went back to the baggage car and, all the way into Denver, listened to items about the people cut in half by the Zephyr on Tiptree's portable radio.

# _____Twelve_____

THERE WAS A MORGUE wagon, driven by a surly fella by
the name of Potter, waiting at the station. He didn't
tell me his name; I had to read it off the license fixed
to the sun visor with rubber bands. He didn't ask for
any help with the body part, just lifted the bundle up
in his arms and carried it over to the wagon.

Walter Bosley, the medical examiner, acted like he
was glad to see me when I arrived at the morgue. He
was in the main room cutting somebody up.

_Every big city in America offers a lot of such work for
those who like it._

"McGilvray's office called to say I should expect
you," he said. "What's that with your ear? You got a
passionate girlfriend?"

"Somebody took a shot at me," I said. "It's nothing
much. I washed it myself."

"Needs a bandage and maybe a little antiseptic."

He was getting cotton, a bottle of antiseptic, and a sterile bandage out of a glass-fronted cabinet. "Sit down on this stool over here."

I handed over the two property envelopes. "You forgot to take these along," I said, sitting down on the stool.

"Oh? Well, throw them over on the table there."

"Aren't you going to lock them up?"

"What for?" He looked at me over the tops of his specs like he already knew something wasn't quite right. "There something valuable in there?" He soaked a piece of cotton in the antiseptic and dabbed it on my wound. It stung like hell and I let him know it.

"So, is there?" he said.

"Not that I know about. But somebody might have had cause to tamper with the evidence."

"I thought those envelopes just had the personal property of the accident victims in them. You have reason to believe it wasn't a case of misadventure?" He slapped a sterile pad and some sticky tape on my ear.

"There's always a chance it could be something else," I said.

He went over and picked up the envelopes, checking the seals and the hasps. "Somebody's been at this one."

"I opened it up to count the money in the clip."

I told him about the amount of money and how the bills were arranged and what we made out of that.

"You've got a lot of faith in people doing the same things in the same way, or even the same person doing

80

the same thing in the same way, each and every time,"
Bosley said.

"Well, I know there're always exceptions, but most
of the time you've got to go with the averages. But
what I want to tell you is that I made that slit a little
wider to get the money out and then sealed it up
again, but it'd been slit open and the change removed
before I got to it."

"This have something to do with your getting
shot?"

"I interrupted the fella while he was at it."

Potter wheeled in the lower half of the man on a
gurney. He looked like he was ready to burst out
laughing.

"Something funny, Potter?" Bosley said.

Potter didn't answer.

"You want some lunch first or you want me to get
right to it?" Bosley said.

"If I'm going to watch, I think I'd rather eat after
instead of before."

"It's all in the mind. When we go we're nothing but
dead meat."

"On the other hand," I said.

"That's right. On the other hand there's the faces.
Almost every one of them looks a little bit like
somebody you know."

He draped the remains and got ready to go to work.
He was all efficiency and business. I could see he
wasn't the type to crack wise and drop cigar ashes in a
cadaver's guts.

While he took samples of this and that, he mur-
mured more to himself than to me, occasionally

raising his head and voice a little so the overhead mike would record his findings. There wasn't much.

When he was finished he called Potter in. "Put this poor bastard on the same tray with his top half, Potter. Did you ever find out what was so funny?"

Potter hunched his shoulders, shook his head, and looked hang-dog.

Walking over to the restaurant after he'd washed up, Bosley said, "I don't like that man. Potter, I mean. He gets pleasure from things a man shouldn't get pleasure from. Sometimes they're the only type we can get for the job. Not always, but sometimes."

They knew him at the chop house. We were shown to his regular table.

He ordered a steak with the trimmings and I got a plowman's lunch of black bread and cheese with a bowl of soup to start.

"You want to read the report when it's typed up or do you want me to give it to you like they do on television?" Bosley said.

"I'll read the report, but I'd like to hear it now."

"Male cauc, five feet eleven, one hundred seventy pounds, brown hair going to gray, florid complexion . . ."

"How's that? He was bled white."

"Subcutaneous characteristics. The number of capillaries under the skin. Also he had a lot of broken veins in his nose and cheeks usually associated with a ruddy face. And booze. He was a red-faced man who liked to drink.

"Teeth stained. Heavy smoker. Barrel-chested. He

suffered from pulmonary fibrosis and bullous emphysema."

I shook my head and smiled, letting him know he was losing me, and said, "I've heard of emphysema, but this other?"

"Related conditions. They go together. One is hardly ever found without the other. One will predominate. His emphysema was advanced but not so advanced as to incapacitate him. Not yet. That was in his immediate future."

I showed my interest.

"You want to know more?" he said. "You a heavy smoker?"

"I was, but I kicked it eight years ago. I'd still like to know more."

"You want the pathology?"

"I'm interested in the symptoms at his stage of disease."

"Severe shortness of breath and coughing, particularly after any exertion or under stress. Sputum is tough, tenacious, and mucoid. Not infrequently, bloody streaks'll be present. Chest pains. Marked weight loss as the disease progresses because the patient may be unable to eat without severe discomfort since swallowing demands momentary inhibition of breathing. I think he was beginning to experience some of that. No swelling of the feet or hands. That would indicate a late stage and the onset of heart failure."

He paused and jerked his head at my plate. "How do you like the soup?"

I stirred my spoon through the okra and shreds of

stewed tomato, then pushed what was left of the soup aside and started on the bread and cheese.

"Teeth," Bosley said.

"What's that?"

"I'm no expert in forensics. We've got people in the police lab for that, but you can't cut up as many and as varied as I have over the years without learning a trick or two. Besides being so badly stained, the subject's teeth were in bad condition. Suffered bad teeth all his life. That was evident from the number of fillings in his mouth. A few of them were gold made the way they haven't made them in this country for over half a century."

"You'll have to tell me," I said, on to the fact that Bosley liked his little stalls and pauses, his little drama before dropping the shoe. Liked to have somebody ask the question so he could deliver the answer like turning on the lights at a surprise party.

"Gold foil. Dentist fills the cavity he's cleaned out with layer after layer of gold leaf and tamps it down with a wooden peg and a mallet. Old technique still used in Europe, parts of Asia, and the Soviet Union. I'd say the man was a foreigner."

We were finished with the meal and having coffee. I took out my handkerchief and untied the corner. I put the nickel down on the table between us.

"This fell out of a pocket."

"Whose pocket?"

"I don't know."

"Why are you carrying it around or is that a long story?"

"It's no story at all except I get absentminded sometimes."

"You want me to put it in the envelope with the rest of their stuff?"

"I'd like you to take a look at it."

He picked it up, hefted it as though he were estimating its weight, then turned it over and over in his blunt fingers, putting his head down close, checking it out through the bottom half of his bifocals. "Odd sort of nickel. Its color for one thing. More like dental amalgam than nickel. These marks for another. What do they mean?"

"I don't know. You got any ideas?"

"Could be letters from some foreign language. Like Cyrillic, you know?"

"Well, no, I don't."

"Or they could be chemical symbols. My chemistry's a little stale."

"Or electrical symbols?"

"Could be. You want me to take charge of this?"

I picked the nickel up. "You don't mind, I think I'll just hold on to it for a little while."

"What are you going to do next?" Bosley said.

"Go back to Akron and see if I can help find the rest of that young woman."

I ended up paying the check, Bosley saying it was better for the railroad to foot the bill for our professional conference than for the taxpayers of Denver County to do it.

# Thirteen

I WORK OUT OF Omaha because it suits me, but the Burlington Northern begins in Chicago and ends in Denver where the tracks of the Denver and Rio Grande Western take up the route to Salt Lake City. There's offices at both ends.

I grabbed a cab and was over at fourteen-o-five Curtis inside twenty minutes. The dispatcher, Henry Frye, was on the phone. He waved me to a chair alongside his desk. When he hung up he leaned back and grinned at me as though I was the prize hog at the state fair.

"Well, aren't you the one," he said.

"Aren't I the one what?"

"Bodies cut in half. I mean that's doing it, that's really making the news."

"Well, for God's sake, Henry, I didn't cut them up

86

myself. I didn't plant those bodies on the right of way so we could drum up a little publicity."

He kept on grinning and shaking his head as though I were a proper wonder. "The phones don't stop ringing."

"They don't?"

"Inquiries about your whereabouts."

"Oh?"

"Newspapers. *Chicago Sun Times* and the *Examiner. Denver Post. Omaha World Journal.* Magazines. *People. Newsweek. Penthouse.*"

"*Penthouse?* For God's sake."

"*Time. National Enquirer.*"

"That's enough."

"Television stations."

"Eeeenough."

"And the head office," Henry trumpeted, pleased to be sitting across from a man being picked out and plucked up for fame, no matter how momentary or fleeting.

"The front office?"

"Oh, yes."

"Why'd they call you?"

"They're calling everybody, Jake. Calling everybody up and down the line wanting to know if anybody's seen their favorite gumshoe."

*I wished Bess were there to tell him nobody called detectives gumshoes anymore.*

"You really got to tell people what you're up to," he went on.

"Well, here I am."

"I ain't the front office, Jake. I ain't even your office in Omaha."

"You been in touch with Omaha?"

"Oh, Silas Spinks called too."

"What did he say?"

"Said he was looking for you."

"He say anybody else was looking for me?"

"Like who?"

"Like anybody from the state police."

His grin got so wide I expected it to split his face so his jaw'd fall off. "Oh, yes. The troopers inquired after you."

"How about the feds?"

"Them too? Oh, yes, the G-men called. You're an important man."

"You want my autograph?"

"You want to call Chicago? You want to call Omaha?"

"I don't think so."

"I didn't think you would."

"How come you think that?"

"Because this case could make you famous and you don't want anybody to drag it away from you."

"Why would I care?"

"Two reasons, Jake." He raised his hand and stuck up a finger. "Because you're like a dog what gets his teeth into a bone and'll die before he lets anybody take it away." He stuck up a second finger. "Because solving these murders'll raise your already substantial reputation with the ladies by a considerable amount."

"I didn't call them murders. Why do you call them murders?"

He raised a third finger. "Because you wouldn't be hanging on so tight if you weren't pretty sure that's what they are." He watched me for a minute, then added, "So you're not going to make any calls?"

"I don't think so."

"Not even to your boss?"

"Not right this minute. And you can do me the favor and tell anybody who calls that you haven't seen hide nor hair of me." I stood up. "By the way. Who told you that the coroner over to Akron was out looking after a sick cow?"

"Well, it would've been his wife, I suppose, wouldn't it?"

"I don't know that he's got a wife. I think I'll use your phone after all."

I called Akron, looking for George, and got Bess on the phone.

"George is out making up another search party," Bess said. "The state police are joining in."

"I think you can answer this question I've got."

"Go ahead, Jake."

"Is Howard Freeman married?"

"No, he's not, Jake."

"Nothing going on between him and Dixie Hanniford, is there?"

She laughed. "I imagine that Howard, shy as he is some ways, and romantic too, would fancy someone a little more delicate—prettier—than Dixie. Younger too, I'd say."

"How about Millie down at the Donut Shop?"

There was a long pause.

"What is it, Bess?"

"Well . . ."

"Yes, go on."

89

"I don't like to be just another gossip clucking away."

"This has to do with an investigation into the deaths of two people," I said, assuring her my interest wasn't idle.

"Well, there's been some talk about Howard and Millie. Only talk, you understand? But what would it have to do with those poor people if Howard's playing around with a married woman?"

"I don't know, Bess, I really don't know. But you go around collecting straw long enough, first thing you know you've got a haystack."

# Fourteen

I DON'T OWN A CAR. That might seem foolish in this day and age, but one of the reasons I thought about working for the railroad when I was nineteen or twenty was the vision of all that free travel on the trains. It didn't work out quite the way I dreamed it, though I've seen about all of this country that's available by rail. However, by and large, I really only know the towns, cities, burgs, and villages along the Burlington Northern right of way. I sometimes feel like the whole 1,042 miles is my true hometown.

But being without a vehicle of my own isn't always satisfactory. I often get the feeling that I'm being pinned down by timetables. I had some hours to kill before I could catch the 8:20 back to Akron. I didn't feel like hanging out in the business offices or around the station or in some saloon, so I called up a friend.

Harriet Lawry is an artist who lives in a warehouse loft on a street along the South Platte River between the Denver Union Stockyards and Riverside Cemetery. If you go out and walk across the street, you find yourself leaving Denver and Denver County and going into Commerce City and Adams County. Besides the perfume of the stockyards, there are nights when the breeze blows in from the sewage disposal plant over by Emerson Street. Rents are cheap.

Unlike Janel Butterfield, Charlotte Shumway, and Maggie Wister, Harriet can't cook worth a damn. I said I'd stop for some groceries and cook her a meal, and since I didn't feel like lugging a brown paper bag full of lettuce and beans on the public transport, I went and rented a car. Besides, I figured it would be a legitimate expense charged against the investigation along with the lunch I'd had with Bosley.

I also bought the *Denver Post*. It's a morning paper and had the news about our discovery of the other half of the male body plastered all over the front page. There was an old picture of George when he was a Denver cop and my name figured prominently in the subheads. I folded it up and put it in with the groceries for more careful reading when I got to Harriet's.

Then I drove over to the nearest branch library and killed three hours trying to make sense out of the marks on the nickel. I went through chemistry, physics, electricity, and biology but couldn't turn up anything that exactly suited. After a while my head was so filled with these little symbols that I doubted I'd recognize one of them if it did pop up.

Driving over to Harriet's, I felt almost like your

average householder doing the shopping, then going home from work to eat with the wife.

I climbed the stairs and rang the bell.

The speaker beside the door said, "That you, Jake?"

I said it was.

"Come on in," she said.

It was nice and warm inside the huge loft. Just as well, because Harriet was bare naked, standing in front of an easel and a pier mirror, working on a full-length self-portrait in oils.

"Let me turn the edge on this tit," she said, "and then we can sit down and you can tell me why it's been a month since I've seen you."

"Did you miss me?" I said, putting the groceries down on a huge plank table near the sink, stove, and refrigerator which roughly marked off the kitchen area.

"I miss my cat when I don't see him for a while," she said.

"Still not giving your heart away, I see." I took the newspaper out of the bag.

"I'm giving damn near everything else away," she said, and laughed.

I sat down and looked at the charcoal drawings and watercolor sketches taped up all around the brick walls. There were clay and plaster sculptures of Harriet in the nude on stands, boxes, and tables all over the place.

She laid down her brushes, threw on a thin wrapper, and pushed back her red hair with both hands. "What do you think?"

"I think I'm drowning in a sea of tits and ass."

She put one knee on the couch alongside my thigh,

bent over, grabbed my cheeks in one big, strong hand, pinched my lips into a pucker, and kissed me. "My pal," she said. She sat down beside me and surveyed the artwork she'd done. I took a longer look myself.

Some of the female figures in the drawings and statues were struggling in the embrace of some creature or other, a bear, wolf, dog, or a lizard of monstrous proportions. From the expressions on the faces I could see, I knew that sometimes the embrace was affectionate, sometimes vicious.

One in particular grabbed my attention. In it the struggling naked woman and the beast were so closely clasped to one another that some of the lines separating them had dissolved. They were toppling over into empty space. It was as though they were trying to become one creature, falling to a single death they would share.

"You're getting very deep, Harriet," I said.

"Are you planning on staying the night?"

I raised my eyebrows at her as I handed her the folded newspaper.

"I don't read those things."

"You watch the morning news on TV?"

"I got sick of all the bad news and violence so I threw my set out the window."

I unfolded the *Denver Post* for her and tapped the front page.

"There's your name, Jake," she said. "Does that mean you're famous?"

"It means that I've been busier than a cat scratching and it's not about to end today."

"I don't want to read it, Jake. You tell me."

I told her all about finding the bisected body,

thinking it was one person, finding out it was two, then finding the other half of the man, while she blinked at me and shook her red hair out of her face every once in a while. She was breathing a little hard.

"You've got to stay over," she said.

"Harriet," I said, "I hope this story I just told you didn't upset or excite you."

"Well, I'm not weird, if that's what you mean, but what do you think makes nurses so horny?"

"I didn't know that was true."

"Well, if it's true, it's because of all the death and misery around them. They want to do something life-affirming. Besides, after what you've been through, I just wanted to help you erase those horrible pictures."

"That's a very generous thought, Harriet, but I really don't think I can stay the night. I should be getting back to Omaha and consult with my colleagues in this matter. On the other hand, I've rented a car, which should allow me to make my own schedule."

"What'd you bring for dinner?" she said.

"You want to eat right now? It's not even four o'clock."

"I just want to know. I've been so busy I haven't had much more than bagels and coffee in a week."

I told her what I'd brought with me.

"Okay, we'll erase your bad memories first, then we'll have dinner."

# Fifteen

I WAS LYING ON my back on the mattress on the floor under the giant paisley shawl Harriet used for a bedspread. She was lying on her belly with her face pointing my way and her red hair fanned out across the pillow. It was the lovely quiet moment after. I should have been floating along in it like a leaf on a river, but the thoughts we'd just tried to erase wouldn't go away. George was tramping out there along the right of way looking for the woman's other half. Maybe he'd already found it.

I reached out for my trousers to get my address book out of the back pocket, thinking I'd give Akron another call. But first I had to blow my nose. When I pulled the handkerchief out of my pocket, I could feel the weight of the nickel tied up in the corner.

I unwrapped it and brought it up closer to my eyes,

shifting my head on my pillow so I could get a little extra light on it.

"Are you getting up to start dinner?" Harriet said.

I looked down at her. When I didn't answer her right away, she opened one eye. "I say, Jake, are you ready to get up and feed me?" She saw the nickel in my hand. "What's that you've got there?"

"A nickel with some marks stamped or carved on it."

"Let me see," she said. She got up off her belly, turned herself around, and sat back against the wall. I gave her the coin. She gave it a careful going over. "Gypsy *patrin*."

"What?"

"Gypsies haven't got a written language. They read and write the language of whatever country they're living in. But they've got a long list of signs just for themselves."

"Where'd you learn that?"

"I've known a lot of different people. I had a friend who played the fiddle and had lovely dark, curly hair as black as tar."

"Did he teach you how to read these marks?"

"The secrets of *patrin* are jealously guarded from the *gaje*," she said, flashing me a sideways, impish grin.

"Don't be cute. I know what's *gaje*. You and me and everybody who's not a gypsy. I'll bet I've had my hands on more gypsies than you have."

"But not for the same reasons," she said, giving me a wink.

"You still know this fiddler with a head like a two-lane blacktop?"

"I haven't seen him in years."

"What did he teach you?"

"I think the triangle with the curved bottom means traveler. These two marks could simply be the Roman number two."

"How about the triangle with the line through the top?"

"If I ever knew, I don't remember."

*It wasn't much but it was something to chew over.*

# Sixteen

I DECIDED TO STAY the night after all. Around eight o'clock in the morning I got up and went over to the morgue to pick up a copy of the final autopsy report including the analysis of the stomach contents.

"Sausage and sauerkraut," Bosley said.

"Plenty of that in Chicago."

"What time does the train pull out?"

"Two-forty P.M."

"He ate it on the train, then. Stomach empties out every four hours, give or take half an hour. Takes eighteen hours, generally, from ingestion to elimination."

I took out my timetable and made a quick calculation. "Means he had the sausage and kraut in Lincoln around midnight. Train would be in the station for fifteen minutes."

"You think he could've ordered sausage and kraut in Nebraska at midnight? Then consumed it in fifteen minutes?" Bosley said.

"Not unless there's somebody does hot delivery off the platform at that hour."

"And they sure to Goshen don't serve sausage and sauerkraut on the train at any time."

"So he brought his meal along?"

"I'd say."

"Sandwiches maybe, but I never see people bringing hot dinners with them," I said.

"Not Americans anyway. Americans take sandwiches or snacks, like you say."

"There was that Fritos package in his pocket," I reminded him.

"But there were sausages and sauerkraut in his stomach. Corn chips too. He had them a long time after the hot food and just a little while before he was killed. Europeans carry hot meals to eat when they travel on buses and trains. Especially the ones from places like Poland and Czechoslovakia."

"You keep getting back to that. The teeth. Now this business with sausage and kraut."

"I'm just telling you what I found and what assumptions we could draw from the facts, if we wanted to."

"Well, it's certainly something to think about," I said.

Bosley looked satisfied. "The FBI called, looking for you."

"They say what they wanted?"

"I thought they were about to say, but they didn't say. You know how they are. They play their cards very close to their vests. Especially the ones from CI-three."

"What the hell is CI-three?"

"FBI counterintelligence squad."

"They tell you they were from this CI-three?"

"I surmised. You don't know much, do you?"

"Well, I don't know about any CI-three. How come you know so much about it?"

For a minute I thought he was going to lie to me and act like he'd had secret dealings, but he thought better of it and said, "Read it in a magazine."

I didn't say anything but "Oh," which meant I didn't put much faith in the existence of top-secret organizations that were bandied about in magazines.

"Well, you're supposed to call them," Bosley said, acting a little disgruntled as though I were deliberately trying to spoil his fun.

"I'm on my way back to Akron. I'll do it from there."

"As you please. I delivered the message." He frowned and stuck his head between his shoulders like a bull about to fight. "So all this doesn't tell you anything?"

"All what?"

"The gold foil fillings, the sausage and sauerkraut, CI-three looking for you and acting coy about it?"

It told me something, but I wanted to know what it told him. "I've got ideas. You got ideas?"

"It suggests to me that the sucker with the gold foil fillings and the hot lunch was a spy."

"And how about the woman?"

He hesitated. "I'll have to think about that," he said.

# Seventeen

THE DRIVE BACK TO Akron took me just under two hours. I wondered if I could justify the extra rental on the car. I'd meant to take the nine o'clock the night before. When I didn't, I figured I might as well get Bosley's final report. After that it seemed foolish to hang around Denver for another day waiting for the next nine o'clock.

When I pulled into Akron at two o'clock in the afternoon, George wasn't in his office. The female deputy on the desk told me he was still out with the search party looking for the missing half. "He was out there yesterday too, but he had to come back in around midday for the inquest."

"Freeman called an inquest yesterday?"

"That's what I said."

"That was pretty quick."

"I don't know about that. He's the coroner and I guess he's got the authority."

"Did the jury bring down a verdict?"

"Short and sweet. Death by misadventure."

The way she said it, I could see the shock and excitement about the corpses had just about died down in Akron. The city papers and television stations were still playing the story up, but it was just an abstract horror a long distance removed from them. In Akron, where the bodies had actually lain all ripped apart, the sensation and notoriety were wearing thin.

"Howard Freeman out with the searchers?" I asked.

"I expect he would be. He's got an official interest."

"But not much enthusiasm for tramping around railroad tracks. You know where he lives?"

She went to a Rolodex and found his file card. She wrote down an address on a three-by-five. "You know how to get out to Danver Road?"

"You'll have to tell me."

She took a map of the area out of a box, found the spot and made an *X*. "Right there. About five miles outside the city limits."

I looked at the little map and then up to the big map on the wall.

"That folder doesn't have the detail the big map does," she said.

"I just had the same thought. Looking at this one in my hand reminded me of something I saw but didn't know I saw."

She nodded like she understood I was just talking to myself.

I went over to the big map on the wall. I'd wondered at the time about any roads that might run along the right of way. I expected there might be one, the one that Freeman told the dispatcher was blocked by an unsafe bridge, but I never expected there'd be two. The second road was not much more than a fire road cut through the pines. But there it was, just over the rise that climbed up from the gully on the other side of the tracks above the river. There it was, a high road that could get anybody who wanted to risk it in a storm from Akron to the Zephyr.

When I started for the door, the deputy said, "Hey! You better watch where you step."

"How's that?"

She grinned. "The town's crawling with newspeople. There's even a couple of fellas walking around with cameras on their shoulders."

"It's the price you've got to pay for fame," I said, and stepped out the door practically into the arms of a pretty young woman wearing a corduroy skirt that had to cost three hundred dollars, a fringed leather jacket worth five, and a two-hundred-dollar pair of boots.

"Excuse me, ma'am," I said, and tipped my hat.

I hadn't gone very far when I caught on that she was walking right alongside me stride for stride. I stopped and she stopped.

"My god," I said, "I didn't know I was so attractive to pretty women like you that all I had to do was bump into them to have them follow me all over town."

"Well, you've got a way about you. . . ."

She waited but I didn't give her any help.

"You got a name I can call you?"

"Jake."

"Well, Jake, my name's Karen Olliphant. I'm from out of town."

"I figured."

"How did you figure?"

"The ladies around here don't dress like you dress for everyday. But then, they don't have to appear on television like you do, do they?"

She seemed pleased that I'd recognized her.

*I hadn't, but why tell her that?*

We started walking stride for stride again.

"You recognizing me makes us practically friends, doesn't it, Mr. Hatch?"

We stopped.

"Hatch? I didn't say my name was Hatch. I said my name was Jake."

"That's right. Jake Hatch."

"How do you figure?"

"When a man with eyes like yours walks out of the sheriff's office as though he had a purpose, I'd say he had something to do with the law. I'd say that maybe he was a railroad cop. And I'd say that anybody who was a railroad cop, in Akron, and named Jake had to be the Jake Hatch who found the severed bodies."

"I wasn't alone," I said.

"I understand that. And I understand you're not alone now and that you'll be even less alone in the near future. A sensational story like this, everybody wants to get into the act. So before the rest of the wolf pack finds you, brings you down, and bleeds you dry, I'd like to interview you."

"I'll talk to you, but not on camera," I said.

"Why not?"

"Because like you say, a sensational story like this, everybody'll be watching. They'll see my face and I'll be useless for my job after that. Every grifter, cheat, pickpocket, and thief'll see me coming when they work the trains."

"Okay. Off-camera. But I can quote?"

"Come on over to the Donut Shop and I'll drop quaint midwestern sayings in your ear."

# Eighteen

MILLIE WAS BEHIND THE counter in her pink uniform and white apron, her yellow hair fluffed out all around her face. She didn't look like apple pie, more like an ice cream sundae, sweet and filling. A little goes a long way. If you compared the two, Millie was the sundae and Karen was an apricot mousse. Expensive and understated, but very choice.

They smiled at one another like cats and ladies do.

"I see you're back, Jake," Millie said, as though we were old friends.

"How's Howard, Millie?" I said.

Her expression went through half a dozen changes, like flickering shadows in a mirror, and she said, "How would I know about Mr. Freeman, Jake?"

"I just thought you might've been giving out coffee when the search party left this morning and you'd know if Freeman was with it."

"Oh, sure. Well, I didn't do the coffee and buns this morning. Calvin got up early for a change. He did it."

"Didn't mention Howard being with the search party or not being with the search party?"

"I don't think he'd have any reason to pick Mr. Freeman out for special mention. What can I get you?"

I looked at Karen.

"Just coffee," she said.

"I'll have coffee and what kind of pie?"

"Apple and cherry."

"Home-baked?"

"I wish I could say yes. From the commercial bakery over to McCook. Cherries are canned, but the apples are fresh this time of year."

"I'll go with fresh," I said, motioning Karen to go ahead of me down the aisle to the last booth.

"You want me to heat it and put a slab of butter under the crust, Jake?" Millie asked.

"I would." We settled into the booth and I took another look at Karen.

*Pretty women are one of the great pleasures in life.*

"Deputy said the town was crawling with reporters and cameramen. I don't see them."

"A rumor came back that the search party'd made another discovery. They all thundered off to be first on the scene."

"What makes you say rumor?"

"It's the third time that word came back today."

"Do you think you'll know when somebody brings back the right word?"

"I don't much care. I've got a crew out there on the tracks. I'm looking for something else."

"What's that?"

"An angle."

Millie brought the pie and coffee.

"You have a way with all the ladies, don't you, Jake?" Karen said, when she saw the size of the slab of pie.

"I appreciate them and I think they know it. What kind of angle?"

She shrugged. "Maybe I should say color. Texture. Background. You know, 'Murder on the Railroad.' 'Machine of a Fading Era Still Takes Lives.'"

"There it goes again," I said.

"Goes what?"

"Somebody calling it murder. Two people fell under a train, probably because of some crazy accident, and everybody wants to see murder."

"You don't really believe that, do you, Jake? I mean the business about some crazy accident."

"There's no evidence to prove otherwise," I said, digging in my heels like a mule.

"But you don't really believe it?" she insisted.

"I suppose not, but that's not a quaint quote."

"I'll respect that. I won't use it. You tell me what I can and can't as we go along."

I cocked my head as though I thought she were working the shell game on me.

"I mean it. I have an idea we'll be seeing each other again, Jake, and I want to play fair right from the start."

I went through the whole thing again, leaving out conjecture, like the business about the teeth, sausage and kraut, and the marks on the coin that could've been gypsy *patrin*. She was a good listener who asked sharp questions, some of which I hoped would get me thinking along some track I hadn't tried before.

When I was finished, she nodded.

"I'm not going to hint at murder on tonight's broadcast, Jake. I'm not going to play a sensational horror for more sensation. I'm not even going to mention your name more than once or twice."

"I just heard a cash register," I said.

"Everything's got a price. We both know that."

"I didn't have to give you anything. I didn't have to even talk to you."

"But you did, so that's that. I'm going to soft-pedal the murder angle and that's good for you. In return I want you to give me anything you get first—"

"Not exclusive?"

"Just first."

"If I can."

She leaned back and looked me over in a way that was different from the way she'd looked at me so far. "You're out of an era, Jake."

"You mean I'm an old man? A relic?"

"You're fishing for compliments. You're not old, you're ripe. A man doesn't have to be very old these days to become a relic. But I didn't exactly mean that. I guess I mean that you're a railroad man. It's written all over you. I guess I mean that the railroads won't be around much longer and when they're gone, I wonder what will happen to you."

"I guess I'll go hang out with old cops and firemen and circus clowns."

"You're a goddamn poet, Jake."

"I'm glad you noticed."

# Nineteen

I FOUND FREEMAN'S FARM with no trouble at all. The house was a good-looking two-story clapboard sitting on the lee side of a swell in the land and further sheltered by an ancient apple tree. A half a dozen outbuildings, including what looked like a pretty new tractor and machine shed, clustered around it like chicks around a hen. A long cottonwood windbreak marched like a file of soldiers across the land about a hundred yards northwest, on the weather side. There was a barn and a silo closer to the cottonwoods than to the apple tree.

I stopped the car at the fork in the dirt road, one leg of which climbed the gentle rise to the yard in front of the house and the other of which went down to the barn.

I got out and stood there with the breeze combing my hair and washing my face. It was still warmer than a fall day should've been, but the cider tang of cold weather was just under the surface.

*Indian summer never did last more than two or three days.*

There were no cows grazing on the hillsides. No bull in the paddock. The fields on the other side of the house where winter feed should've been grown had been cut but there were no stacks of hay under canvas.

It was a pretty picture of a farm not much used.

There weren't even any chickens in the wire pen and no clucking from the henhouse.

I stood there for a long while looking at the house on the hill under the apple tree and then the barn and silo in front of the cottonwoods. Nothing moved. The only life I saw was a hawk riding the thermals overhead.

I walked up to the house about halfway, my head pointed toward the door but my eyes looking out from under the brim of my hat at the windows on the first and second floors. Then I cut across the grass to the path leading to the barn and silo.

There was a window in the side door, too dusty to let me see much. There was a lock dangling from the staple but the hasp hadn't been engaged, so I shoved the door open and stepped inside. The smell of cattle still lingered but it was plain that none had sheltered there in a long, long time. There were new spiderwebs and the long strands of broken ones drifting in the air above my head.

I turned around to leave when I saw the metal disk and handle leaning against the wall beside the door among the handles of some muck rakes and hoes. A pair of earphones was draped on a small bracket on the handle of one of those metal detectors once used for clearing minefields and used more recently for combing beaches.

The sound was no louder than the creak of a board in the breeze or a mouse overturning a corn cob. When I turned my head I saw a slight drift of dust falling through the cracks in the boards of the loft, falling like flakes of gold in a beam of sunlight.

I climbed up the ladder to the loft. Freeman was sitting on the floor by the door, grinning at me. "This is private property."

"Not much to steal," I answered, as though I took his remark for a little bit of kidding and was kidding right back.

"Just being nosy?"

His grin may have changed or maybe I just saw it differently, but all at once his smile wasn't very pleasant.

*Were all his smiles just cardboard fakes pasted on to draw attention away from his eyes? They were cold eyes, flat and watchful.*

"Just wanted to ask about the inquest," I said. "How come you went ahead and held it without the testimony of the witnesses on the scene?"

"What for? I had your deposition, didn't I? It came in handy after all. I talked it over with George first and he said go ahead. He thought it might help to get the whole damned thing out of the newspapers and off the television so he could go about his business without tripping over people."

"Didn't help much, did it? Press all over the place."

"Thick as fleas. Who told you I held the inquest?"

"The deputy at the sheriff's office."

113

He got up off the floor with the same graceful ease he'd shown hopping into the baggage car. There was a moment I thought he was going to attack me, but he just said, "He tell you I was here?"

"She. She didn't know."

"So you took the chance I'd be off with the search party. Thought you'd have yourself a little look around."

"No," I lied. "I didn't think you'd be off with the search party. I figured you'd have had enough of that."

"One time was enough for me," he agreed. "When I saw your car coming, I was afraid it was somebody sent by George to get me."

*It was about as lame an excuse for hiding as I'd ever heard.*

"So, here I am. If you came to see me about something, speak up."

*One second he was being chatty and the next belligerent, like a damned teeter-totter. I knew from past experience that when a fella starts acting like that he can be dangerous.*

I started backing down the ladder. He started coming down right after me, not facing the rungs the way farmers do but clambering down face forward like a sailor.

*Sailors tuck their cigarette butts in pockets and folds, just like soldiers do, whenever they're in an area that needs policing.*

"Well, I just did speak up," I said. "I wanted to know about the inquest."

*That was a pretty lame excuse too.*

"Was it decided murder and mayhem by person or

persons unknown or was it death by misadventure or—"

"The deputy didn't say?"

"She didn't seem to know."

"I thought everybody got the word. Just goes to show."

We both had our feet on the barn floor by now. I started walking to the door with him right behind me. When I got there, I nodded to the metal detector.

"I haven't seen one of those since I took a vacation to Florida and saw the old men out early in the mornings hunting for coins and jewelry on the beaches."

"Go to Florida often, do you?"

"Well, no, just the once. But that thing just reminded me of that one time. Get much use for it around here?"

He knew exactly what I was doing with all my talk about Florida beaches and old men looking for tourist treasure, knew that I was trying to put him in a box and make him scramble for a story that would explain having such a device on a farm. For a second I could see that he was about to tell me to go to hell with my little games and traps, but then he shook his head as though amused and said, "Plenty of use. I go through these fields with that thing and pick up all sorts of old rusted machine parts and busted sections of barbed wire that work themselves up to the surface. Cows get that crap in their stomachs while they're grazing, it can do a lot of damage. Don't do a man's foot any good if you step on some of it, neither."

"That's pretty clever, using that thing like that. I'd never have thought of it."

We left the barn and were out in the clean air.

"Get the idea when you were in the army?" I went on.

"Got the idea combing beaches down in Florida," he said.

When I looked at him, he was grinning at me in that challenging way again.

"So you took a vacation down there too?"

"I was with the circus for a time when I was young. We winter-quartered there."

"So you were never in the army?"

"Oh, I was in the army. The navy too."

"How's that?"

"Army has boats and ships, you know. I was a soldier but I was part of a ship's complement. We going to swap war stories? Which one was yours?"

"Korea."

"That was a police action."

"Which was yours? Vietnam?"

He nodded.

"That was a disaster."

# Twenty

THE CHICKENS SCATTERED OUT of my way as I drove into the backyard at McGilvray's. Bess was standing on the stoop with a broom in her hand. She came down a couple of steps and the screen door banged shut behind her. She turned to look at it as though it had startled her, and I knew she'd been daydreaming about something.

*Standing in the sun, remembering what it had been like when she was a young woman waiting for her new husband to come home? Or back further still when it would have been her father coming home to supper?*

A cold wind kicked up some dust and fallen leaves. Autumn was back.

"Hello, Jake. Have you had anything to eat?" she asked as I got out of the station wagon and started walking toward her.

"I had a big breakfast in Denver."

"That was hours ago. Come inside. Will a chicken salad sandwich do you?"

"If you've got any of that soup left on the stove, that'll do me just fine, Bess."

She seemed pleased that I liked her soup. I took the broom from her hand. She watched me do it as though she'd forgotten it was even there.

She laughed. It sounded sad but brightened her face, which was still very pretty.

"George wants to hire a cleaning woman to come in."

"I'd let him."

"I never worked outside the house, you know? Not before I married or after. These big changes in the lives of women came too late for me. I mean, even if the arthritis would let me go out to work, I'd be afraid to. My home is all I've ever had by way of work."

"And taking care of your father for years after he was widowered, and being a cop's wife for forty years, and raising three kids in Denver, and growing vegetables out back here, and keeping chickens, and making quilts, and . . ."

She laughed again, with greater pleasure. It was a silver sound. "You do know how to charm," she said.

"After I have my soup, I'm going to take down your screens and put up your storm windows and doors," I said.

"George had it on his calendar for this week and then—"

"So let me earn my supper. I sure as hell can't sing for it."

I was almost through with the windows when

George came back. Dixie Hanniford was riding with him. She got out of the prowl car first.

Without her hat on she looked younger and somehow prettier, more like the young girl she must have been before the hard life of farming and the harsh wear of the years had thickened her.

I came down off the ladder as she went around and helped George out of the car, taking his whole weight, when he stumbled, with hardly a flinch. He was wet clear up to his waist.

"You need a hand?" I said, hurrying over.

"I can manage him, I think, but if you want to give him your shoulder it might ease his leg a little better."

Bess was making soft noises of concern as she stood there holding open the door. Nothing like panic—she could see he wasn't wounded—more like the gentle clucking of a mother at a child who'd fallen out of a tree.

"It's nothing, Bess," George called out. "Twisted my knee climbing back up the slope from the river."

"George figured out where the rest of that poor girl might be," Dixie said. "It was a bad place and he just had to lead the way."

"Well, I don't know who else should've gone first."

"Somebody considerably younger," Dixie said, and tossed a wink at Bess.

George turned his attention to me as the only way of politely cutting off that kind of talk. "I didn't expect to see you back so soon."

"There's a couple of things needs talking about. You talk to the FBI?"

"They've been calling but I haven't called back yet."

Dixie and I let go of George in the mud room and went on into the kitchen.

While he took off his boots and corduroys, Bess hovered around him, plucking up pieces of clothing as fast as he could shed them until he was down to his long johns. He didn't protest even though she winced once or twice. He knew enough not to refuse the loving attention. I got a blanket off the bed and brought it back so George could wrap himself in it. He backed up to the stove, making a funny sight, while I poured him a cup of hot coffee.

"You got something to lace it a little?" I said.

"I'm temperance," he said.

"Since when?"

"Oh, since a long time."

Bess came back with a pair of trousers, a flannel shirt, wool socks, and sheepskin slippers.

George turned his back and Dixie turned her head while he dressed, though George in long johns was nothing to see.

Bess started setting out soup and bread then. Plain, sturdy food that filled a body's stomach right down to the toes.

*There was that about marriage. Somebody always there to do the little things for you, and you for them, with scarcely a word passing between you. That kind of knowing couldn't grow very wide or deep in the kind of relationships I enjoyed.*

"Don't set out a plate for me," Dixie said. "I've got to get back to my own place."

"How about just a cup of coffee?"

"Not even that. I'll want to take a nap when I get home."

"All right, then," Bess said, but still Dixie didn't leave.

"The other half of the woman'd slid all the way down the slope into the stream," George said. "A miracle it didn't catch on a tree or bush."

"Probably just happened to fall on a patch where the underbrush had been swept clean by a rockslide," Dixie said, wanting her share of the story.

"Anyway, she was way the hell downstream, almost to Platner."

"Treacherous land around there," Dixie said. "All shale and scree, slippery as mercury."

George looked up at me while putting on a sock and said, "Young woman. Badly battered. She might have been very pretty once, but . . . Well, you'll see. After I eat and get warm, we'll drive down to the station. You'll see."

He went back to the other sock, as though he didn't want to talk about it anymore with the ladies there.

Dixie said, "Well," and put her hands on the table to lift herself up.

Her hands gave me a start. They weren't all banged up and short-nailed like you'd expect a farm woman's hands to be. They were red and chapped with cold, but smoother than any at the work should be, the nails longer than most and painted red.

She saw where I was looking and grinned, taking her gloves from her pocket and drawing them on. "Vanity, vanity," she said.

# _____Twenty-one_____

WHILE BESS SAW DIXIE Hanniford out through the mud room, I started telling George what I'd found out in Denver as he settled down to finish his meal.

I told him about the postmortem findings, about the fillings in the teeth and the sausage and sauerkraut in the belly.

"From that evidence Bosley figured the man was a Middle European and a spy."

"Well, I suppose that's as good a thought as any," George said.

Bess came back and sat down again.

"How does Dixie keep her fingernails looking that good?" I asked her.

"Oh, she likes to dress out like she's a working farmer but she's big-city. She came here with a pocketful of cash and bought the Clinton place next to the farm Howard Freeman bought."

"Just a gentleman farmer?"

"Well, lady farmer," Bess said, laughing a little.

"Same thing," George said. "Plenty of money. Sick of the city. Longing for the simple life. Buys a farm for more than it's worth. Hires plenty of help. Spends a fortune fixing up the house. You ought to see it."

"Ought to see *her* when she's out of that mackinaw and work boots and into a negligee and slippers," Bess interjected.

". . . then goes around in a brand-new but dirty pickup with a dog in back and a shotgun in the cab."

"Dixie's so open and up front about having fun playing the part, nobody much minds. She'll probably get sick of it after a while and go away to try something else."

"How long has she been around?"

They looked at each other again, didn't say a word for a minute, then said, "A year. No more 'n that," in practically one voice.

"Are she and Freeman very good friends?"

"You mean more than just friends?" Bess said.

"Whatever."

"As far as I can tell they're just good neighbors."

I took the nickel out of the corner of my handkerchief and put it down on the table. "I've been asking around about these marks."

"You find out anything?"

"I've got a friend says they're gypsy," I said.

"Could be hobo signs," George said. "Trick is to read them, whatever they are and whoever made them."

"Let me have a look," Bess said. Taking the nickel

in her poor twisted hands, she brought it up close to her eyes. "The first little triangle could mean telling fortunes with cards."

"How could you know something like that?" George said, openly surprised.

"Annie McMonigle taught me a little one sunny afternoon."

George made a sound halfway between a cough and a grunt.

"What's the matter?" I said.

"George doesn't approve of Annie McMonigle," Bess said.

"It's not a question of approving or not approving," George said. "She owns a house."

"Hardly a house. Nothing but a shack. Not much more than a garden shed."

"Well, it's shelter. The fact is she has a little money from somewhere and no need to beg the way she does. No need to gather up all the junk she collects, stuffing it into that shack until she can't live in it and the city has to send the fire department in there once a year because she's turned it into a prime fire hazard. No need to sleep in people's basements or in doorways. I've come near to breaking my leg a dozen times this year alone stumbling over her curled up in the back doorway of my office, right there by Shultz's dumpster."

"The poor old thing picks through the vegetables he throws out."

"He's told me a hundred times that all she's got to do is ask and she can have all the ripe fruits and vegetables she wants to lug away."

"Well, she's too proud to ask, isn't she?"

*I could understand being too proud to ask for a handout but not too proud to scavenge.*

"Just who, may I ask, is Annie McMonigle?" I asked.

"One of Akron's oldest citizens," Bess said. "She was a child at the turn of the century and saw Halley's comet twice."

"She could be in her nineties," George agreed. "Pesky woman. Charges housewives for telling their fortunes."

"Harmless," Bess said.

"Well, I don't know. I've had complaints about things gone missing after Annie's been in the house."

"Pesky or not," I said, "maybe this old woman knows something that could be useful."

There was a knock at the door. Bess went to answer it.

"Annie," she said.

There was an old woman standing on the stoop. She was wearing layers of skirts, half a dozen blouses and sweaters, an old shawl with a man's felt hat over it jammed down almost to her ears, and fingerless gloves. Her feet slopped around in a run-over pair of men's brogues with the laces gone, tied onto her feet with bits of twine.

"Hey, George," I said. "Maybe there's something in this business about gypsies reading minds and telling fortunes."

"Hell, she's just doing her weekly rounds," George said.

Annie's clever eyes caught sight of George, who'd turned around to face the door, and then of me.

"Somebody's talking about me," she said.

# Twenty-two

ONCE GEORGE INVITED HER in, he treated her with all the courtesy he gave to every other woman. We both half stood up, bent at the waist, until she'd taken a seat at the table.

Without asking, Bess served her a bowl of soup and a thick slice of bread slathered with butter and jam, then drew her chair up beside her.

"Do you mind?" Annie said, and before anyone could say did they or didn't they, she popped out her false teeth and put them into the pocket of her topmost sweater.

"These aren't my eatin' teeth," she lisped. "These are my sportin' teeth." She slurped up a few swallows of soup without even testing how hot it was, soaked a piece of bread, butter and jam to soften it up for her gums, popped it into her mouth, chewed, and smiled in sheer satisfaction. "How can I help you, General?"

"Don't call me General, Annie. You can call me Chief, Mr. McGilvray, or George, whichever suits you best, but stop turning me into a military man."

"You remind me of a soldier I knew in my youth," she said. "He was a general. Or maybe a colonel. Memory falters."

"Have you lived here in Akron a long time, Annie?" I said.

"Long enough."

Bessie put her hand over Annie's free hand, hers looking older than Annie's, twisted as it was with the arthritis, and said, "Annie introduced herself the first day George and I arrived in this house."

"Were you on the road much when you were young, Annie?" I said in a soft, friendly voice.

She looked at me as though she'd like to tell me that she knew the smell of butter, but for Bess's soup she'd put up with as much of it as I wanted to spread.

"From one end of the country to another before I was married."

"And when would that be?"

"Before your time."

"Was your family Romany? You don't look like Romany."

"How would you know what Romany look like?"

"Oh, I've seen gypsies in my time. Even knew one or two."

"Which is it?"

"Which is what?"

"Did you know one or two?"

"Well, I knew a whole family when I was a boy. Knew two brothers best. They were Manush."

"Valsikanes? Piemontesi?" she asked.

I shook my head once, saying I didn't know what she meant.

"French circus gypsies?" she said. "Italian gypsies?"

"I don't know much about the different types. What sort of gypsy are you?"

"My people were Kalderash."

"But you didn't marry a gypsy?"

"No, I married a cowboy."

"You have any children?"

"Twelve." She'd been looking at me all this time, glancing at her plate only when she filled her spoon. Now I saw her eyes fill up with tears.

"All living?"

"All dead by now. I lived too long. There's nobody left to lay me outside to die, or wash my body, or put a gold coin in my coffin, or toast me by name at the grave."

"Oh, you know there'll be someone there—I'll be there—to do that for you, Annie," Bess said. "I don't know about laying you outside to die, though."

"Okay, you can forget that part. You can forget about the gold coin too. They come very dear nowadays."

"I'll make the toast if I'm around, Annie," I said.

"How can you do that? You don't even know my name."

"Why, it's Annie McMonigle isn't it?"

"That's just my *nav gajinkano* name. The name I use with people who aren't gypsies. I have other names."

"What name's on your birth certificate?"

"My name isn't on any birth certificate. Not on any

school record or census list, neither." That seemed to please her. "Some names might be on some old police records but they won't be my names either."

"You were arrested?"

"Oh, plenty."

"What for?"

"Telling fortunes. Stealing. Working the *bujo.*"

"What's that?"

"Switch-the-bag. See, people are sick or having bad luck. They come to me. I say, 'Have you been given a large sum of money lately?' 'Well, yes I have,' some people say, or, 'Not lately, but I've got some in the bank.' 'That's the trouble,' I say. 'That money's got a curse on it. Bring it to me and I'll take the curse off it.' They bring me the money, and right there in front of their eyes, I sew it into a piece of cloth. Then I get them to look elsewhere for a second. I do switch-the-bag and give them a package in the same cloth which has nothing but cut paper sewed up in it. I tell them to hold on to the package unopened for a week or ten days. Until I know I'm going to be out of town." She laughed. It was more like the cackle of a hen. "Then I tell them they can open it. That's the *bujo.*"

"That sounds pretty slick."

"Not so slick. It brought the FBI down on us. They could make it a federal crime because the people doing it were crossing state lines." She made a whooshing noise through her nose that was meant to demonstrate her disgust at such lack of understanding.

"You think they should just let you go on stealing?"

"Taking from the *gaje* isn't stealing unless you act too greedy."

"Do you really believe that?"

"I'll tell you a story," she said after finishing the last bite and carefully wiping her mouth on the corner of the tablecloth. "Jesus was going to be crucified. A gypsy blacksmith was ordered by the Roman soldiers to make four nails, three for the hands and feet and one for the heart. The gypsy didn't want to make the nails but the soldiers whipped him until he did. When he delivered the nails, he swallowed one and told the soldiers he'd lost it. When God saw that he'd swallowed the nail meant for the heart of Jesus he said, 'Gypsy, you're free to go and travel anywhere and you can steal your food and take what you need to live.'

"That's why gypsies travel and why they steal."

"Do you still steal from the *gaje?*" McGilvray said.

"When I stopped traveling, I stopped stealing," Annie said, looking him hard in the eye, knowing damn well that George halfway believed the tales told about her stealing by forgetful or deceitful housewives.

"Did you ever pick pockets, Annie?" I asked.

"It's against my religion to tell you that," Annie said.

*She was having fun teasing me.*

"Did you ever work the trains picking pockets?"

"Oh, sure, I had my *wortacha.*"

"*Wortacha?*"

"Partners."

"Have some more soup, Annie?" Bess said.

McGilvray looked daggers at Annie and then at her plate. Not that he begrudged her the food, he wasn't like that at all. It was just I could hear his mind working, telling himself that Annie was like a stray cat. You start feeding one, and first thing you know, you've got a cat whether you want one or not. He could see it. Pretty soon she'd be coming regularly for supper, then for lunch, and before they knew what'd happened, she'd be sleeping in the woodshed summers and in the furnace room winters. Maybe even in the guest room.

"I've had a sufficiency, thank you," Annie said, and popped her teeth back into her mouth.

"I can't stand sleeping in the same place every night," Annie said as though she'd read George's mind too. "Even now when I've grown too old for the road." Her speech was clear and lilting, her voice much younger than her face and body.

George handed her the nickel. "Do these marks mean anything to you?"

She scarcely glanced at it.

"It's a gypsy will," she said. "Part of one, at least."

"How do you make that out?" I said.

She gave it a closer look.

"This first mark means fortune because this last triangle with the line through the top means that a master died."

"Master?"

"The chief of a tribe. The leader of a band. Or maybe just the head of a family. The father. The master."

"What about the two lines between the triangles?" Bess asked.

"That could mean a lot of things. Two of anything. Like two horses. Or it could mean that two people are meant to share the fortune—or whatever—half and half. Or it could mean that whoever was given this

131

coin was being told to take second place to another who was the first heir of the chief who died."

She wiped her mouth on her sleeve with a motion that was almost delicate.

"I don't think it's horses," she added. "That was in the old days. Gypsies don't have much to do with horses anymore, especially not here in America. They travel in trucks. They use the trains and planes. The old ways die. You'd like all gypsies to be sedentary gypsies."

"Are you a sedentary gypsy?" I asked.

She stared at me with old, watery eyes that were wiser than any creature's I'd ever seen except maybe for a tortoise I'd known once long ago.

"I'm an excluded gypsy," she said. "When I married outside the tribe, my family wouldn't have me anymore."

"How old are you, Annie?" I asked.

She grinned, showing her white false teeth.

"Old enough to chew hay," she said.

I didn't know what else to say. After a couple of minutes Annie got the idea she was no longer wanted and asked to be excused. Bess told her to come with her first because she had a warm sweater she wanted to give her.

When they'd left us alone in the kitchen, McGilvray said, "That old woman's probably got thirty sweaters. Now that it's blowing cold and winter's coming on, she'll get thirty more."

"I suppose it makes Bess feel good."

"I suppose."

When Bess and Annie came back into the kitchen, the old woman had a bundle of old clothes in her arms. She shuffled to the door, stopped, and with the air of somebody who was doing a great, though reluctant, service for the authorities, turned to George and said, "On the other hand those marks could just be somebody's calling card."

Then she went out into the cold.

Bess was grinning when she came back to the table. "Well, now you know more than you did before Annie came to supper."

"But what we know doesn't seem to be doing us a hell of a lot of good," George said.

"Gypsies and spies," I said.

"What's that?"

"Gypsies and spies are a little too exotic for my taste."

"If we've got to have killings, and I had my druthers, I'd like it better if it was two drunks going at it in a fight over a barmaid," George said. "But it seems to me, we haven't got any choice in the matter. Read the papers. This country's got as many spies running around as ticks on a hound dog's belly. Gypsies too."

"Oh, I know gypsies," I said. "I see them on the trains and nab them working their games in the stations. Know about them passing through towns, oiling down houses, claiming it'll preserve the shingles. Read about them flying here and there in groups, stealing radios out of cars, and busting into parking meters."

"So," George said, "if it turns out it's spies and gypsies we got, we'll just have to accept the fact that they're the nuts that fell off the tree."

"What bothers me most is that we've got both these unusual, out-of-the-ordinary, types involved in the same case of death by misadventure. I wouldn't mind so much one or the other, but both is . . ." I groped around for a word.

"Too much of a muchness," Bess said.

"Too much of a muchness," I said, nodding. "Well, I guess we'll just have to learn some more about them so they won't seem so peculiar."

I had a brief picture of Harriet and her drawing of the merging woman and beast. That reminded me about trains passing in the night, one going east and the other west. I took the timetable out of my pocket.

"Have a look at this," I said.

George moved his chair over a little and so did I. Bess got herself in the middle so she could see as I put the timetable down between us.

I put the tip of my finger on McCook, Nebraska. "There it is."

"There's what?" they both said.

"The only place the woman could have got off the train going east and then got on the train going west."

"Both trains pull into Holdrege within twenty-five minutes of each other," George said.

"But the train going east pulls in later than the one going west. The train with the man on it would have been on its way before the one with the woman on it arrived at Holdrege. McCook's the only place that makes sense. See, right here? Eastbound arrives at one fifty-three A.M. Westbound pulls in two hours later."

"How big is McCook?" Bess asked.

"It's a town of about seven, eight thousand."

"Anything around there?" George asked.

"Prairie."

"Military installations? Missile silos?"

"There's the SAC base at Omaha," I said.

"That's better 'n two hundred fifty miles from McCook," George said. "If it was two spies meeting, why didn't one just go to where the other was? Chicago, maybe. Or Denver. Instead of all this fancy dipsy-doo train hopping in the middle of Nebraska?"

We were all quiet for a while, staring at the timetable as though we could scare it into giving up some secret. Finally, I folded it up and put it back in my pocket.

"You want me to take that girl's other half to Denver?"

"Are you going back there again? You're like a Ping-Pong ball."

"I'm going to McCook first. Then I'm coming back so I can stop at Fort Morgan before I drop the body in Denver. I'd like to find out if anybody remembers seeing that young woman on any station platform, or getting on or off any train between Denver and McCook."

"You want to go down to the station now and look over what we found?" George said.

"If I've got to, I guess I've got to."

135

# Twenty-three

LOOKING AT THE YOUNG woman's face was a lot worse than looking at the face of the middle-aged man with the gold foil teeth. She'd fallen down the mountain into the gorge and been battered against the rocks as the white water tumbled her along.

Her head and torso, half wrapped in the rubberized groundsheet they'd carried her in, was lying on a bench in the back of the garage where the sheriff's cars were kept.

"She was snagged around a tree trunk in the flood," George said. "When I first saw her, it looked like she was alive, her arms holding on to the roots and her head turning from side to side as if she was trying to look over her shoulder and cry for help." He cleared his throat. "Then I remembered she had no bottom half."

She had thick black hair that had probably once

been her vanity and her pride. I could picture it combed out, haloing around a pretty face. Now, the lights had gone out in it. It was a sodden mass of old crepe paper, fingers of it clinging to her white neck, strangling her even though she was already dead.

Her eyes were half open. Even with the film of death over the pupils, they were as black as coal and glittered as though alive.

"She liked a lot of jewelry," I said, noting the heavy necklace lying on her bosom, the rings on the one hand that had been exposed when I'd lifted the groundsheet away, and the loop earring that tugged at the lobe of her ear.

"One earring's been torn away," George said.

"God, that river roughed her up," I said.

"It's a wonder she wasn't battered worse the way that water was running."

"Has Howard Freeman had a look at her?"

"I had the office put a call into him as soon as we brought her back. Dixie Hanniford said she'd stop by his farm on her way home and tell him."

"No kind of farm," I said.

"How's that?"

"I was out there today. Freeman has a pretty farm but nobody's working it."

"I've heard he's letting the fields lie fallow because he intends to change over to some experimental crops."

"Like what?"

"Like that plant they're starting to grow commercially for use as insecticide."

"Pyrethrum?"

"That's the stuff."

"Meanwhile, isn't he supposed to be keeping some cows?"

"I wouldn't know about that. I hear the farmers talk, but I don't listen to half of what they say. You've got to remember I'm not a local, born and bred. I'm a big-city boy. I know about keeping the peace. I don't know about cows."

"Well, he was supposed to be sitting up with a sick one the morning it took the Denver dispatcher an hour or more to rouse him. Five o'clock in the morning and the man said he was out in the barn with a sick cow."

"Farmers get up at the damnedest hours," George said.

"But I didn't see any cow out there," I said, raising my voice some because George didn't seem to be getting the point. There was a rap on the door. "No damned cows at all!" I repeated for emphasis . . . and the door opened. Freeman was standing there with his toothy grin and his foggy glasses.

"Talking about cows, are you?" he said. "Is that what you were doing prowling around my place, Hatch? Looking for a sick cow?"

I didn't bother to answer and he didn't expect me to. He was just sticking it to me. He looked down at the girl.

"You know her?" I said.

"What's that?" he said, turning his head sharply, looking at me as though he'd like to hit me.

"Have you ever seen her anywhere before?"

"What makes you ask me something like that?"

"What's so strange about asking a question like

138

that? Unless you're always at the farm with your sick cows, you might take a trip to Denver or Omaha. Here or there. I just asked you, like I'd ask anybody else, did you ever see her. On the off chance," I said, flaring up.

"Goddammit, don't mind me," he said, backing off fast. "I'm nothing but nerves. There's a lot about this job I could do without."

"Looking at things like this shaves everybody's nerves pretty fine," I said, wanting to ease my bad temper as well as his.

"Find anything on her?"

"No pockets in the blouse or jacket. Just the jewelry she's wearing," George said.

"Anybody ever found her purse?" I said.

They both looked at me as though that were a thought that had never occurred to either of them.

"That won't be easy to find," George said.

"Maybe if we got one of them metal detectors like the beachcombers use," I said, one eye on Freeman. "All kinds of metal things in a woman's purse."

"What good would a detector do with all that steel track and tie spikes?" George said.

Freeman gave me his best grin.

"I don't know a lot about how those things work," I said, "but I'd venture a guess that they can be tuned down pretty narrow. If the purse is there, it won't be caught between the ties because we walked the track miles in each direction and somebody would've seen it. It would have fallen one side or the other, far enough away from the rails so they wouldn't interfere with any signals."

"There'd still be all kinds of scrap. Tin cans. Old bed springs. Who knows what all the way people throw junk along the right of way," George said, thinking all we were talking about was a way to facilitate another damned search, this time for a woman's pocketbook.

"Close to towns and cities, but not out there in the hills," I insisted.

"We'll see about it when you get back, Jake," George said. "I'd hate to ask anybody to go tramping around that treacherous ground again, looking for nothing but a purse."

"Where you off to?" Freeman said.

"Denver. The morgue."

"Aren't they coming to get her?"

"I rented a car in Denver yesterday and I've got to get it back," I said. "I might as well take her with me."

Freeman smiled at me in the way he had that made him look like a nasty little boy and I knew there'd never be any real peace or friendliness between us.

"Make sure you don't get yourself stopped along the highway. Trooper finds her in your trunk, they could throw you in jail and maybe punch you once or twice before George could come get you out."

"I never break the speed limit," I said. "But I never let up on the gas until I get where I'm going, either."

He turned away. "Say hello to Bosley for me." Then he stopped in the doorway and turned back to grin at me again. "About the cow. You were looking in the wrong barn. Farmer who put that cow barn down by the cottonwoods was a damn fool. There's a shallow there collects cold air like a pond. He must have had his troubles with cows going down with slow fever and

seized knee joints. I built me a cow shed, big enough
for six, the other side of the house where it's sunny
and sheltered. Ask around, Hatch. You'll find out I'm
experimenting with special cows just like I am with
special crops." He walked out and shut the door.

"Well, I guess you just got told," George said.

# _____Twenty-four_____

IT'S NEARLY TWO HUNDRED road miles to McCook, and when you get there you wonder why you made the trip. There's nothing much to see there except the train station, a commercial street sixteen blocks long and one block wide that serves the farmers and ranchers round about, a John Deere showroom that tries to make tractors and cultivators look like Cadillacs and Lincolns, a water tank, a movie house, and the steeples of half a dozen churches, including a Baptist church which, for some reason nobody can explain, is the only steeple that has a belfry full of crows.

There were three automobiles and a pickup truck parked in the hard-packed red dirt that passed for a parking lot alongside the station. I put my car around the corner where the station cast some shade. Cold as it was, I knew the trunk of a car could heat up pretty fast and I feared what that would do to what I was carrying in it.

Dearborn Simmons, the station agent, was inside, plowing through a pile of paperwork at his desk. He was wearing paper cuffs he'd clipped to his sleeves and a green celluloid visor, the likes of which I hadn't seen, except on him, in twenty years. Green roller shades covered the windows and filled the place with cool, watery gloom.

"Help you?" he said.

"Your eyes going back on you, Simmons?"

"There's a glare in here," he said.

I leaned over the counter, sticking my face halfway between here and there.

"Jake Hatch," he said. "What the devil you doing in McCook? Don't tell me. Come to see Charlotte Shumway."

"Come to see you."

"What about?"

"You heard about the tragedies along the road just outside of Akron?"

"It's in the city papers and on the television. Bodies cut in half. My god. That's not going to do the reputation of the railroads any good, under attack by the congress for not paying its way like they are. You got anything new to tell me?"

"Not a thing. What I wanted to know is, have you had any trouble with gypsies around here lately?"

"You mean like with earrings and red bandannas around their heads?"

"Well, I don't know about that. Gypsies dress just like everybody else these days, I suppose."

"Well, I see the men wearing belts made out

of coins and the women in those long skirts, don't I?"

"So, you have seen some around here lately."

"Not that I noticed."

"No complaints about pockets being picked?"

"None that's been complained to me."

"The day before the accident along the right of way, you see a young woman wearing trousers get off the eastbound Zephyr?"

"That time of the morning I'm asleep on the cot unless somebody comes in and rings the bell at the counter."

"You mean there's nobody up and awake?"

"How many tickets do you think I sell at four in the morning?"

"Somebody must ride the trains out of McCook."

"Not so's you notice. Besides, they'd probably already have their tickets bought in advance."

"Well, all right. This young woman, though, would've got off the eastbound at two o'clock and hung around the waiting rooms until the westbound pulled in at three fifty-five."

"Now, why the hell would she do a thing like that? Get off one train and get on another going back the other way at that hour of the morning?"

"Because she was making a connection with somebody maybe?"

He looked up at the ceiling. "I wonder. Did I see a young woman like that?"

"You mean you weren't asleep all that time?"

"Well, I don't know that, do I? I mean who remembers on this day or that day, in the middle of the night, did you get up to get a drink of water or take a pee. I can tell you I don't remember anybody ringing the bell and asking for any service. But . . ."

"But what?"

"I'm trying to remember did I get up, shuffling around half asleep, you know, and did I see anybody in the waiting room or on the platform."

"Not on the platform. It was storming."

"I did get up once to water my horse," Simmons said, putting up a finger, finally sure of it.

"And you saw somebody?"

"Not here in the station. I looked out the window in the front door as I passed it on the way to the toilet just at the second there was a lightning flash. I think I remember seeing somebody, I don't know was it a man or a girl, walking across the street toward the diner. Whoever it was had their head down with something over it to keep from getting wet. That's what I think I saw."

"Is that diner all-night?"

"No. But they're open until around four. Back when Amtrak was making a special effort with public relations, they made a deal with Cooley Gaines to stay open as a convenience for any passengers might be taking the trains. I don't have to tell you they gave up pretty quick but Cooley stays open anyway."

"Thank you," I said, starting for the door.

"Might not be open now. I tried half an hour ago and Cooley's brother-in-law, Wylie Pope—lazy son of a buck, wouldn't have the job except Cooley figures he'd have to support his sister and her kids anyway— hadn't opened up yet. Cooley'll strip his hide when he finds out but he won't fire him, even though Wylie's usually late opening maybe twice a week and sometimes don't open up at all. You see Cooley's trying to work it out how he can—"

"I think I understand," I said, putting my hand on the latch and opening the front door. "Cooley's trying to figure out how he can cut his losses since he can't turn a profit on the work he gets out of Wylie."

"That's about the size of it. By the way. You'd better come back here before you leave town and call the front office. There's people looking for you from one end of the line to the other."

I said I would and walked across the street toward the diner. Halfway there I saw that the sign in the door said CLOSED. Cooley's brother-in-law, Wylie, was still dogging it.

I could wait, or I could go over and visit Charlotte Shumway and then come back.

I drove over to Charlotte's house to see if I was too late for lunch and too early for tea.

When I pulled up in front, Charlotte was already at the front door. She put her hand palm out at me about the time my right foot hit the top step of the stairs leading to the porch.

"Is that an Indian welcome, Charlotte, dear?" I said.

"That's a message that maybe you shouldn't come any farther."

"Is something wrong?"

"You've not been around in six months, Jake."

"Five months, two weeks and two days," I said, using a trick of calculation and memory that never fails to impress the ladies.

"I'm flattered you should know to the day when you saw me last, Jake, but that's not what I mean."

"What's not what you mean?"

"I'm not disturbed because it's been such a time since you came visiting. I knew you were a traveling man when we met. I'm just pointing out the fact that it's been a long time and a lot can happen in a long time."

"Like what?"

"Like I've taken up with another gentleman, Jake. A local gentleman who's not a traveling man."

"It's serious?"

"We're engaged."

"I don't see a ring."

"Well, pre-engaged."

"You mean you have an understanding?"

"Sort of an understanding."

"I expect an understanding should make a fella feel very secure, especially when the understanding he has is with a woman as good and true as he must know Charlotte Shumway to be."

"Butter melts in the sun, Jake."

"Under the crust," I said almost dreamily.

"What's that?"

"All your undeniable charms notwithstanding, Charlotte, it's a wonder how I can never get within nose distance of your front door without thinking about apple pie, warm from the oven, with a slab of butter under the crust."

Charlotte was no fool. She knew I was flattering her shamelessly. But I'd long since learned that such outrageous flattery carries a certain power. It's daring. Like going up to a strange woman in a bar and kissing her as though the pull had been so strong that even a slap from her or a punch in the mouth from a boyfriend would be worth it. I've done that once or twice, in my youth, but I haven't tried such shenanigans in years. Age takes its toll. I just use flattery now, assuming that the flatteree knows that the flatterer wouldn't take the bother over someone they didn't care about a lot.

"I don't think Wilbur would—"

"Wilbur?" I couldn't help blurting out.

A little ice formed on her eyes and mouth. "Yes, Wilbur. Something?"

"Just startled me. That was my favorite cousin's name," I lied.

The ice melted but I could see the temperature only had to drop by one degree for it to come back again. "I don't suppose Wilbur would have any call to mind if I invited an old friend into the kitchen for a piece of homemade pie," she said.

"With butter under the crust," I said, stepping onto the porch.

It wasn't long after I'd finished two pieces of her pie and praised it to the skies that we were holding hands across the kitchen table with me saying that I'd been thinking lately of settling down. The view I had in mind was cuddling with Charlotte just one more time before her engagement became official and she was lost to me forever.

If I'm giving the impression that I'm a jackrabbit, pouncing on every stray doe that passes by, it would be a wrong one. Believe it or not, I'm much alone in my nearly empty flat in Omaha and it's only on occasion that I'm out among other people. Especially females. Charlotte's going and getting almost engaged without my even knowing is proof enough of that.

I sometimes believe that any charm I may have with the ladies lies in the fact that they know I'm a traveling man, more or less, and can be depended upon not to linger too long after we've had our moment.

In any case, things were progressing. My finger was making circles in the crook of her elbow, and I had her trying to read the truth in my melancholy eyes, when her phone rang.

It was Dearborn Simmons, the station agent.

"I hope I didn't interrupt nothing," he said.

"Only a little gossip between old, dear friends," I replied, throwing Charlotte a little bonbon while telling Simmons to speculate no further.

"You were asking about gypsies?"

"I was."

"Three of them just stopped by. Two men and a woman."

"How did you know they were gypsies?"

"The older man was wearing a fedora and a bandanna around his neck. The younger one had an earring in his ear. The woman wore one of those big skirts and a blouse cut so low I could easy tell her fortune." He laughed like steam escaping from a radiator.

"Half the men in Nebraska wear fedoras," I said. "Farmers wear bandannas to catch the sweat. Nowadays, plenty of youngsters wear one earring. And some of these girls and women on the farm communes—"

*I was looking for an excuse not to leave Charlotte.*

149

"Don't tell me I don't know what gypsies look like," Simmons said. "The men had belts made out of hammered silver coins."

"Did they say anything I'd be interested in?"

"They asked me about that night and about a young woman just like you did."

"What did you tell them?"

"The same thing I told you."

"Did they buy tickets for the train?"

"One man and one woman did. Then they left. The other, the young one, stayed behind. He sat around for a while. Bought himself a cup of coffee out of the machine, then didn't drink it. Finally he asked me was the food in the diner across the street any good and I said it was when it wasn't closed. He went to the door and looked. It was open. He walked across the street and I went to the door to see, and sure enough Wiley, or maybe Cooley—because sometimes, you understand, Cooley gets so annoyed at Wiley that he fires him for a day or two and tries to work both shifts—"

"Never mind that, please, Dearborn. Where's the young gypsy, now?"

"Over at the diner, like I said."

"Well, thank you for calling, Dearborn."

"You're welcome, and you know what?"

"This isn't about Cooley and his brother-in-law, is it?"

"Oh, no, it's about the gypsy. I've seen that fella in McCook before."

I hung up, kissed Charlotte, told her how much I appreciated the apple pie and regretted I couldn't stay and chat. Then I said how I thought she was doing the right thing planning to marry Wilbur.

"You were saying something about settling down, Jake," she said, putting her hand on my arm so I couldn't get out the door.

"Well, as you can see, that's hardly possible. I'm a good playmate but a bad partner, Charlotte."

"Well, gather ye rosebuds while you may," she called after me as I hurried to the car. "You're not getting any younger!"

*She didn't have to go and say that.*

# Twenty-five

I PARKED THE RENTED car in the same spot where the
station still gave some shade, then walked across the
street toward the diner. A big semi with aluminum
sides was parked next to a milk tanker. There was a
Piels sign glowing neon-pretty in the window beside
the screen door, which hadn't been taken down for the
cold weather yet. My mouth was dry and the thought
of a cold beer felt good except I doubted it would
settle very well on top of Charlotte's apple pie with
butter under the crust.

I was dithering inside my head a little because I had
the feeling that the way I handled this meeting with
the gypsy was going to make or break the case.

It was three steps up to the screen door, which
screeched on its hinges when I opened it. I held it with
one shoulder and used the other to open the regular

door. A cozy damp warmth, smelling of bacon fat and coffee, hit me in the face like a wet washcloth and lifted my spirits.

A fella with a white counterman's hat perched on thinning red hair turning white—it had to be Cooley —was standing behind the counter reading the sports page. He gave me a glance but decided not to move until I decided which stool or booth I was going to pick.

There were two men in leather jackets at the counter, driving gloves sticking out of their back pockets, hunched over cups of coffee. One of them swiveled his head around and took a gander at me, but there was nothing about me that interested him so he went back to staring into his mug.

I looked down the right-hand length of the diner and there, facing me, was the only person in the joint who could have been the gypsy. A kid about twenty-three or four, black hair curling all over his head like a basketful of snakes, small gold loop earring shining in his ear. His eyes flicked up at me. I knew the look of the hustler checking out every stray rustle in the brush, looking for a score. His eyes were as black and shining as the girl's. They could have been family.

There was somebody sitting facing him. Somebody who was big and had a pale neck and wore a mackinaw of a pattern I'd seen more than once before. Freeman half turned his head looking for Cooley and the coffeepot while he stuck out his empty mug. I could see the metal bows of his spectacles pressing against his temples. He had his hair cut white-sided in a way you don't often see nowadays, so there was no mistaking him. I wondered why I'd never noticed that about him before. It was the sort of thing a sophisticated but not too clever man might do who wanted to look like a clodhopper.

*I don't know if anybody says that anymore, Bess.*

I stood as still as a hare in a hedge. Cooley looked over his paper at me again as if waiting to see should he serve me first, if I ever made up my mind where I was going to light, or should he just go and give the big, pale-faced man a refill. I don't think I was much more than a fuzz in Freeman's peripheral vision when he noticed Cooley looking at me. He shifted his head another fraction. I was turned around with my back to him and half out the door before he thought to take the bother and twist his whole body around.

"Refill!" I heard him say, just as the screen door slammed behind me.

I got back across the road fast, ducked into the station, and sat down on the first bench inside the door so I could take a minute and think about what I'd just seen.

*What had they been doing when I came out of the cold into the steaming diner?*

They'd been hunched over the table like the truckers had been hunched over their mugs of coffee on the counter. But there'd been something else. Unless I was just wishing for it, I could've sworn I caught a flash of green as money and something brown like a wallet passed from hand to hand.

"You find that gypsy over to the diner?" Simmons called out from the ticket window.

"He's in conversation with somebody," I said,

getting up and looking out of the window. "I'll just wait here until they get through."

It wasn't long before Freeman came out. He stood on the top step buttoning up his mack and putting on his gloves, looking one way and the other, but never looking directly across the street at the window of the station where I stood back watching him through the grimy pane. He came down the steps and went around the tail end of the trucks. A minute later his pickup backed out from behind the tanker where it'd been parked out of my sight. He hit the highway heading back to Akron.

When I walked through the door of the diner the second time, Cooley put down his paper and picked up the pot, staring at me as though ready to make sure I sat down this time and ordered something.

"Hamburger rare. Toast the bun. Pickle, no relish. Mayonnaise, no mustard. Fried onions."

He lifted the coffeepot. I started walking down the aisle toward the gypsy who was looking at me in speculation again.

"Coffee. Milk and sugar," I said.

I sat down across from the gypsy. He didn't protest, just smiled like a man who figured he was about to do some more business.

"You've got good hands," I said. "You been picking pockets and cleaning purses long?"

"That's a hell of a way to start a conversation with a stranger."

"You tell me your name and we won't be strangers."

"Nick Kemp. What's yours?"

155

"Jake Hatch. Mine's real."

I was calling him a liar but he didn't take offense. Gypsies believe lying to a nongypsy is no sin and telling the truth to one no virtue.

"A name's just a convenience," he said. "I'll call you anything you want and you can call me anything you want."

"How about thief?"

He shrugged. The quality of his smile changed. "Why don't you put an egg in your shoe and beat it?"

I made a show of silent laughter and slapped my knee. "The first time I heard that I laughed so hard I fell out of my cradle." I reached into my pocket and took out my badge, cupped it, and stuck it under his nose.

"Railroad," he said.

"You've seen one before."

"Once or twice. When I was on a train. You notice I'm not on a train?"

"You ask your elders about Jake Hatch. They'll tell you I don't roust your people for no reason. I don't hassle them in public and take away their faces. You tell them I said their son, Nick Kemp, refused to talk to Jake Hatch, so now Hatch's going to step on their toes every chance he gets. Search them in the aisles. Doubt their honesty out loud. Tell them the trouble will come from my hand but that it's on your head."

Cooley brought over my hamburger and coffee.

"How's it going, Cooley?" I said.

"Working goddamn double shifts."

"Ought to kick that no good son-in-law out on his ass."

"I would but then my daughter'd give me hell and never let up."

"Son of a bitch. You'll find a way."

"You said it."

He walked away with a little lift to his step as though having somebody know how bad his son-in-law was and how good Cooley was made it a little easier to bear. I knew he was back behind his counter, looking at me and wondering where he knew me from.

"You know why I did that?" I said.

"Did what?" Nick replied.

"Had a little friendly chat with Cooley?"

He didn't answer.

"I did it so that when I start beating up on you he won't step in and take your side or ask those two truckers to take your side. You see, he figures I'm a friend. He doesn't know from where, but still a friend who cares about his troubles. So when I start punching you around they won't jump in to help you and they'll be slow to stop it."

"Railroad dicks are sons of bitches," Nick said.

"We are. Now, what I want to know is what business you had with that fella who just walked out of here."

"What fella?"

"The one with the pale face and the round glasses. The one in the mackinaw who slipped you some cash."

"That a good hamburger?"

"Is that your way of saying you're not going to cooperate with me?"

"You want to talk to the old men, go talk to the old men. What do I care? You think my family'll give me the silence because some *gaje* cop makes a threat?"

I still had half the hamburger left and I hated to leave the rest, but I put it down, finished off the coffee, got up, put down a five, and without waiting to see if there was any change, told Nick to come outside with me.

"Is this when you beat me up?"

"This is when I show you a pretty girl who's not a pretty girl anymore."

He came scrambling after me as I walked down the aisle. "What the hell you talking about? What pretty girl you talking about?"

When I got outside I stopped. He almost ran up my back.

"You missing a pretty girl?" I asked.

When he hesitated, I turned around and crossed the street, heading toward my car.

"Jackson said my friend was in a safe place," Nick said weakly.

We'd reached the sidewalk. I stopped and faced him. "Jackson?"

"That man you saw me talking to in the diner."

"I think he lied to you. I don't think your friend's safe."

"Hey, wait a minute. Wait a minute." He was three shades lighter, all the blood gone from under his olive skin. He turned his head a little sideways as though trying to get a new, clearer angle on me and what I was saying. His mouth wasn't young and hard anymore. It was younger than young and soft, like the mouth of a baby ready to cry. "What do you know about my woman?"

"I think she's dead. I want you to look. Then you can tell me if it's her."

I started walking again and he stumbled along after me, plucking at my sleeve and saying, "Wait. Wait."

We were at the car. I got out the keys and stuck the trunk key in the lock.

"Wait a minute," Nick said. "You're not going to tell me you got somebody in there. You're not going to tell me—"

I lifted the trunk lid.

"—you go around carrying bodies in the back of your car."

I untied the knots on the twine that held the groundsheet around her head while he rattled on about what kind of a person I was playing such rotten jokes.

"You're not going to tell me you got—"

I pulled aside the folds of rubberized cloth and revealed her face.

"Cara! Cara." First it was a shout, then it was a moan. He tried to go down on his knees and gather her in his arms. I threw my arms around him instead and backed him off three paces.

"Don't do that, for God's sake. You'll never forget it if you live to be a hundred."

He turned around and I let go. He stood there trembling. "I'll never forget it now," he said.

"That's her? That's your woman?"

He nodded his head. He said something very softly in a language I didn't understand.

"Your love?" I heard myself say, and he nodded again so I suppose I understood after all.

"You gave her the little book of poems?"

"Yes."

I quickly covered her up again, closed the trunk and locked it. I asked him if he wanted to go back across the street for a coffee or maybe he'd like to find a bar and have a shot of something. He said no. We went into the station instead. Simmons stuck his head out of the ticket window. He was smiling as though pleased to have been of help. He was about to say something but I shook my head and he disappeared.

"I'm sorry I had to do that," I said. "But you let me know you weren't going to believe a thing I said."

"Jackson told me Cara was safe. Did he kill her?"

"I don't know. There was an inquest. They brought in a verdict of death by misadventure." I didn't tell him that the man he knew as Jackson was the man I knew as Freeman and that he'd also been the coroner who'd helped bring down the verdict.

"Misadventure?" He said it as though he didn't know the meaning of the word.

"Didn't you read it in the papers or see it on television about the two people who fell off the Zephyr under the wheels?"

He shook his head. "We don't bother much with newspapers or television. What have they got to do with us?"

"I don't know how you can avoid them nowadays."

"That's what I've been telling the old ones. That's what Cara and me've been saying. These are modern times and things have changed. Why fight it? Why not use it? Why should we go around being different, looking different? Why shouldn't Cara wear pants like the *gaje* women? It even made it easier to work the games. Now, I don't know. Maybe the old ones are right. Maybe it's better we stay apart. I made a mistake. It's okay to clean the *gaje*. It's not okay to go into business with them. Cara and me have been punished."

"Listen to me," I said. "I'm not going to say if it's right or wrong to follow or don't follow the customs of your people. Maybe it's a small thing, but for what it's worth, if your girlfriend wasn't dressed like a *gaje* woman, there'd never have been any mistake about who'd fallen under the train or how many'd been killed. It would've been cleared off the books as a tragic accident and everybody would've forgotten about it. But here I am trying to find out what happened to your woman. And you've got to help me."

What he had to say wouldn't have filled the space on a match cover.

Nick and his girlfriend lived with their families in a nice apartment in a nice building in a nice Denver neighborhood. They kept some of the old style and some of the new. The head of the family, Nick's uncle, decided which was to be which. No newspapers, no radio, no television, because they served the *gaje* world and, like Nick'd said, had nothing to do with gypsies. They played tapes and records on the latest equipment, though. Knew how to wash dishes in sand but cooked in a microwave when they weren't on the road. Traveled in trucks and campers most of the time, but took the jets to this place and that when off on a thieving sweep.

"Jackson got in touch with me through my uncle. He knew I was working the trains from Denver to Chicago."

"How did he know that and why did he pick you?"

"He knew my family from years ago when I was just a little kid. My family worked the circuses and carnivals for a while and he was an acrobat or something."

"So he asked you to do a job of stealing for him."

"At first I told him no," Nick said. "What kind of fool did he think I was, I said, stealing for somebody else.

"He said what it was he wanted stole wouldn't be worth anything to me. He showed me a thousand dollars and said he'd give it to me on the spot and another thousand after we did the job."

"For switching briefcases?"

"Jackson brought one to us. He said it looked exactly like the one the mark'd be carrying. He was right about that but he didn't know much more about it."

"How's that?"

"He didn't know a person, carrying a soft-sided satchel like that, every once in a while could stick it under his arm. They could feel that it's empty."

"So you put a newspaper in it."

"Took it out of the trash basket."

"And the switch went all right?"

"Oh, sure. Easier than we thought it would. Cara dressed like one of them tight-assed *gaje* women going to the office. Suit, shirt, and tie. Carried the briefcase in her arms against her chest. The mark comes walking down the aisle. Starts to cough. Sticks the satchel under his armpit while he reaches for a handkerchief. I bump him and poke it through. It falls on the floor. Cara bends down and does the switch. I shove it back in the mark's hands while she goes around him. The mark thanks me. I follow Cara down to the vestibule where she hands his satchel to me. She turns around and goes back the other way empty-handed. She's supposed to take her seat and get off in Denver. I use the toilet in the club car. I leave the briefcase by the sink."

"Where'd you get off?"

"I got off in Denver too."

"You didn't pull the emergency?"

"Why would I do that?"

"Then you were sitting in one of the cars when I came through making the announcement about the reason for the emergency stop? About the passenger falling under the wheels?"

"Where else would I have been?"

"When you didn't see your partner again, didn't you start wondering where she'd got to?"

"I wasn't *supposed* to see Cara after we pulled the switch. After a game like that you're not *supposed* to make any contact until you know your skirts are really clean."

"You didn't wonder if maybe it was your partner under the train?"

"You said it was a *man* you found along the tracks." He was almost shouting as though defending himself against me. As though I was accusing him of not taking care of the woman he loved. He was saying it wasn't his fault. But he felt it was his fault. I could tell it was running around his head. If he'd taken better care, he might have saved her from whatever sent her flying out into the rain and the dark to get battered and cut in half. At least he could have gathered up the pieces and taken her home.

I put my hand on his shoulder and he didn't shake it off.

"What could you know, kid?" I said. "A couple more questions. I don't like to keep at you, but if we're going to get the person who—"

"Go ahead," he interrupted, not wanting to hear me say it.

"Did your girlfriend carry the thousand?"

"When I got it from Jackson, I put it in my money clip. She wanted to see it, then she wanted to hold it. So I let her take it with her."

"How about the second thousand?"

"It was waiting for me in a coin locker at the railroad station just like Jackson said it would be if we pulled it off."

"When Cara didn't turn up at home, did you report her missing?"

He tossed me a look full of contempt. "You mean to the police?"

"Yes. To the police."

"We take care of our own."

I didn't say anything, but maybe he could see the foolishness of that contemptuous remark mirrored in my eyes, because he started crying and couldn't stop for a long time.

After he quieted down, I said, "So you went out looking for her on your own?"

"All along the route from McCook to Denver. Back and forth. Looking for something. Looking for somebody who'd maybe seen her. Nobody'd seen her."

"Jackson call you to meet him?"

"No. I've been here in McCook since this morning. He just showed up."

"Since when this morning?"

"I came on the train."

"From Denver? That means you've been hanging around here since two o'clock this morning?"

"There's people live at night even in a town like McCook. I thought I could talk to some of them and find out things ordinary people wouldn't know."

"You talked to many?"

"Some. They didn't know anything about Cara."

"You say Jackson didn't contact you?"

"I went to the diner to get some coffee and he came in five minutes later."

"What did he want to see you about?"

"He wanted to know if we took anything else off the mark that we didn't tell him about."

"Had you?"

"We were going to do the 'stumble and switch' and let it go at snatching just the satchel. But the mark was coughing so hard and so long that Cara thought she'd just vacuum his pockets as long as she had the opportunity."

"She didn't get everything because we found some junk in his pockets."

"But not his wallet."

"She got that?"

"Yes. She even got his pocket change. She was showing off for me."

"She pass that to you along with the briefcase?"

"Yes."

"But you didn't leave it with the briefcase in the toilet."

"That wasn't part of the deal."

"What was in the wallet?"

"About two hundred and some dollars in cash. Driver's license. Some credit cards. A gate pass."

"You remember the name on them?"

He shook his head.

"You remember the company name on the gate pass?"

He shook his head again.

"You keep the wallet and the credit cards?"

"I kept it all."

"Is that what you just sold to Jackson?"

He nodded his head this time.

Nick looked at me with eyes that had aged twenty years. "Where you taking her?"

"To the morgue in Denver."

"Are they going to . . ." He didn't have to say the rest for me to know what it was he couldn't ask.

"When you get your friend back, she'll look almost like you remember her," I said. "I'll get her things back for you too, as soon as I can. The book. Her comb. Even the money. Just give me a telephone number where I can reach you. I'll make an arrangement when I get permission to return her things. I'll bring them to you or I'll have somebody bring them to you."

He gave me a number, looking at me sideways as I wrote it down, having more than an inkling that I intended to use him some way, but wanting his sweetheart's possessions back bad enough to go along with anything I wanted without asking questions.

# Twenty-six

BOSLEY WASN'T VERY GLAD to see me. I guess even a medical examiner gets to the point where he starts to lose his immunity to horror.

"I hope this is the last of these packages you're going to bring me, Hatch."

"So do I."

Potter came out to get the bundle from the trunk of the car, the crazy little smile flickering around his mouth.

He carried it inside as Bosley and I stood out in the cold.

"I haven't had any lunch and it's on to supper. She'll have to wait."

"Don't you go home to supper?"

"I did for twenty years. When I was married."

"Are you a widower?"

"My wife left me. After twenty years she left me.

Said she just couldn't stand to smell the stink on me a minute longer."

"Why didn't you quit pathology?"

"I offered but it was too late. You married?"

"No. Never been."

We thought about our mutual solitary condition.

"Well, we could stand here feeling sorry for ourselves or we could go have a meal."

He went to get his topcoat and hat. Then we walked over to the same restaurant we'd eaten in before.

"You know anything new about this mess?" he asked when our plates were in front of us.

I gave him the whole opera word for word, on the off chance something in it would trigger a notion that might prove useful.

"This coroner? This fella Freeman who calls himself Jackson around the gypsies?" Bosley said.

"I've got my best eye on him."

"How'd he know this Nick Kemp was in McCook?"

"Somebody told him when they saw the gypsy boy arrive on the morning train?"

"Lots of people looking for such things in the wee hours of the morning over in McCook?"

Bosley destroyed half his steak before he spoke again. "There's only a few outfits can afford that kind of manpower, Hatch."

"Which one did you have in mind?" I said.

"Well, decide which side you think Freeman is on and take your pick." He looked at me for a long minute and said, "I'm sure you've already thunk it. You've got an interesting technique."

"What's that?"

"You go around acting dumb and letting people

spout off showing how smart they are. Then you pick the ripe berries out of the box."

"It hardly does any good to ask right out what somebody thinks about something," I said. "Even if they haven't given the matter any thought at all, when you ask them, they'll surely tell you something—anything—just so they won't look dumb."

It wasn't much surprise to either of us when we got back to the morgue and found the Feds waiting. That's one of the outfits both of us'd had in mind.

I knew one of the G-men.

*Bess McGilvray would say nobody calls them that anymore. I wish she wouldn't do that—remind George and me that we're moving up closer and closer to the head of the passing parade.*

I knew him because he worked out of the Omaha office and we'd met on one case or another maybe three times during the last three years.

His name was Barry Trask. He had an easygoing grin and a trick of looking half asleep that covered up a very hard nature. He was an efficient man who hated to make a mistake and hated to be wrong.

He introduced the other agent, Martin Janosky, who turned out to be a higher-ranking agent working out of the regional office in Denver. You could tell at a glance that nobody ever called Janosky Marty. He was wearing a shiny gray suit, a lighter gray shirt, a gray satin tie, and shoes with a high polish. He had prematurely gray hair and wore steel-rimmed Photogray glasses. He looked like a dressed-up automaton made of steel, chrome, and platinum.

I introduced Bosley. Janosky smiled briefly and

asked him to please leave for a few minutes, but to keep himself available since they'd want to speak to him by and by. Bosley bristled like an old porcupine and said, "Don't let matters of protocol get in our way here, Mr. Janosky. There's no reason why we shouldn't sit down around the coffeepot and do this the easy way."

"I don't want the interrogation of one possible witness tainted by the interrogation of another," Janosky said.

Trask grinned at me from behind Janosky's back and rolled his eyes up to the sky.

"Witnesses? Witnesses to what?" I said.

"Well, we don't know yet, do we?" Janosky said.

"We're all working the same side of the street, son," Bosley said. "At the moment you're in my neighborhood, so, unless you want to go about this in a more official manner, we'll do it my way. I expect you're smart enough to figure out that anything that comes out in any conversation between you and me would soon be known to my old friend, Jake Hatch, anyway. And vice versa."

"How's that?"

"Because I'd tell him."

Janosky turned to Trask and nodded. That was the signal for us all to sit down. Bosley poured out coffee for everybody without asking, more a peace offering after Janosky's capitulation than a gesture of hospitality.

Janosky asked all the questions. Trask just sat there smiling lazily and taking it all in.

Janosky ran me through the events on and off the

train: the discovery of the severed body, McGilvray's assumption of interim jurisdiction, Bosley's discovery that the pieces belonged to two people not one, the later search for and discovery of the man's lower half and my transport of that part to Denver and the morgue. And then the search for and discovery of the head and torso of the girl and my arrival with it in the back of a rented car. That's where I stopped. I mentioned nothing about McCook and the gypsies.

He wasn't the sort who charmed you into wanting to make his job easier. If the FBI was taking jurisdiction, they could sort the evidence and figure out for themselves what it might mean. I remembered the nickel still in my pocket, tied up in the corner of my handkerchief. I didn't tell him about that either.

He turned to Bosley and got all he'd given me over lunch and a little more. Details that only another pathologist would care to know about. The only time Janosky's expression changed is when he tightened up a little when Bosley mentioned the way the teeth had been filled with gold and the stomach with sausage and sauerkraut and the assumptions Bosley had drawn from those facts.

"What can you tell me about the other body?" Janosky said.

"Female Caucasian. Latin or Mediterranean. I'd say five feet one when I get to measure all of her. A hundred and five pounds . . ."

Janosky turned his gray eyes to me. "How could you think half a woman weighing a hundred and five belonged to half a man weighing a hundred and seventy?"

"In the driving rain along a pitch-black track humping along a wooded mountain ridge?"

"Afterward. Back at the depot in Akron."

"Looking at two human parts, a top and a bottom, who could imagine there was more?"

For the first time he made a little smile, saying that *he* would've thought, *he* would've known, *he* would've been unmoved and unshaken. He passed a hand across his face, wiping the smile away, almost shuddering at the realization that he'd smiled in the first place.

"This is our status as of this minute," he said. "The bodies will remain with you here at this morgue. They're to be put into adjoining drawers and the drawers are to be locked—"

"They don't lock," Bosley interrupted. "We don't have many body snatchers around Denver."

"A federal agent will arrive sometime today to seal them. If he has doubts about the security of this facility, he'll post himself on site until such time as a decision is made about the disposition of the subjects. Dr. Bosley, you are hereby officially on notice that you are not to discuss this matter or any of your findings with any other person unless they carry specific authorization. The mere showing of a shield or government identification should not be considered enough to give anyone access. Anyone must show evidence that they have been informed of this matter and are privy to what is presently known. You may ask questions to satisfy that requirement."

"While the unauthorized person is punching me around the face and neck, kicking in my ribs, or

173

putting a knife to my esophagus?" Bosley said. "What the hell's going on here, son? The least you can do is tell us who the dead man and woman are."

"I can't tell you about the man and I don't know about the woman."

Bosley shrugged his shoulders, sighed, and looked at me as though I might have a clue about dealing with this robot. I gave a little shake of my head.

Janosky turned his attention to me. "You're under the same injunction. Talk to no one about this."

"You've cleared this with my boss, Silas Spinks?"

"We will."

"How about Sheriff McGilvray in Akron?"

"He's been informed." Janosky stood up. "Now, I'd like to officially take possession of the property found on the bodies."

Bosley and Janosky left the office. Trask and I were alone.

"That your boss?" I asked.

"No, but he's senior on this."

"He's got a way about him."

"He's an asshole, but if you ever say I said so I'll call you a liar and a communist sympathizer." Trask grinned and batted his lazy eyelids as though he were about to fall asleep on the spot. "But what the hell, you know and I know that you're going to do what you damn well please, talk to anyone you damn well feel like talking to, stick your nose in where you damn well feel like."

"A man doesn't trust me enough to offer me his confidence, I don't believe myself constrained by his rules."

"While you're telling him to go to hell by doing

whatever it is you intend to be doing, just keep me personally informed if you come up with anything."

"You want to ace him?"

"I don't want to step on any toes, but the name of the game is save your own ass. And if I can come out of this assignment one up on Janosky, why the hell not? So, you'll do me the favor?"

"Tit for tat?"

Trask thought that one over. We could hear Bosley and Janosky in the corridor coming back to the office.

"Where you staying?" Trask said. "I'll call you."

I didn't know what to say, having made no plans to remain in Denver any longer than I had to. "When'll you be calling?"

"Probably not until after seven tonight."

"I have a friend, Harriet Lawry, lives in town," I said, writing down her name, address, and telephone number in my notebook and tearing off the page. "If I'm not there when you call, she'll know where you can reach me. If you get no answer at all, call back here at the morgue. I'll leave a message if I don't connect with Harriet and tell you where else we can meet."

He took the slip of paper just as Janosky walked back in. Trask folded it once, put it in his pocket, and stood up. "Thank you for your cooperation, Mr. Hatch," he said.

We shook hands all around and they left.

As they walked down the hall, I heard Trask murmur, "We'll keep an eye on that bird," just loud enough for me to hear.

175

# Twenty-seven

HARRIET WAS GLAD TO see me. "Twice in one week, that's something."

I kissed her and told her that seeing how skinny she was made me take pity on her, so I'd brought along the makings of a truly great mulligan stew the way I'd learned to make it from the boys in the camps along the Burlington Northern right of way.

Trask called just as we were sitting down to dinner.

"Where'd you like to meet?" he said.

"Where are you?"

"Downtown in a bar near Union Station."

"You taking a train?"

"No. I'm just having a beer. I'll be driving back as far as Akron with Janosky. He wants to personally inform Sheriff McGilvray that we're taking jurisdiction. Funny. McGilvray's been hard to get on the phone, just like you."

"I could get over to you in about forty minutes. I'm finishing my dinner."

"Well, I can cab it over to you in twenty. By the stockyard, isn't it?"

"You know Denver?"

"I've got a map."

"All right, do that. I'll give you exact directions."

"Will your friend be there?"

"Yes."

"That's no good then. I don't want what we've got to talk about broadcasted all over town."

"She wouldn't be interested. But you could be right. She lives in a loft and there aren't any walls or doors, except for the bathroom, and I can't ask her to go sit on the pot until we're through."

"We could ask her to take a bath and then go in and wash her back after we finish our business. I'm making smart remarks, Jake, because I'm still not sure I should go through with this."

"I'm not going to twist your arm," I said.

The line was silent for a long minute.

"I'm checking my map again," Trask said. "I can meet you at the entrance to the cemetery or at the Elyria Park swimming pool."

"Cemetery's better for me," I said.

"Twenty minutes. Go finish your dinner," Trask said, and hung up.

Twenty minutes later, I passed up a second cup of coffee, kissed Harriet, and told her I'd be back for it in no more than half an hour.

A cab was parked outside the cemetery with its sidelights on. The driver glanced at me once, then looked away.

Trask was sitting on a tombstone halfway along the path before the first turning past the entrance gate.

His eyes were closed and, at first, it looked as though he didn't even hear me coming. Then he turned his head a couple of inches, opened his eyes, and smiled. "I was sitting here thinking about how it's going to feel when I'm dead."

"It's not going to feel," I said.

"Let's hope not."

I looked up overhead. The city-shine wasn't as bright in the sky over the dark patch of the big cemetery. The stars seemed brighter.

"Why are you hanging on to this one, Jake?" Trask said. "You'd think two people falling under a train and getting cut in half would be the sort of action you'd just as soon do without."

"Why are you taking jurisdiction?" I asked right back. "You'd think the same two people would be of little consequence to the FBI."

"We developed an interest."

"What took you so long? How come you let it lay in my lap for three days?"

He eyed me like a poker player holding cards in a last-hand, everything-in-the-pot showdown.

"You've got a ride to catch," I said. "If you're going to tell me, tell me."

"The man's name is Bela Mazurky. He traveled on a passport under the name Benjamin May. We think he was a Czech, though he could've been Rumanian, Hungarian, or East German. The citizens of the countries under Soviet domination are different from the Russians but their intelligence services are pretty much the same and all of them are run from Moscow."

"What was he doing on the Chicago Zephyr?"

"He lived in Chicago. He traveled a lot. But almost always east. To Detroit, Pittsburgh, Scranton. Smokestack cities. Sometimes to New York, Boston, or D.C. We figure he was an expert who vetted industrial intelligence gathered by other agents. That's where most of the action is these days. Or he could have been nothing more than a courier."

"He was on his way west."

"That's why surveillance was a little more than casual this time."

"Maybe he was taking a vacation."

"Why not? Spies, government agents, and cops do the same things everybody else does."

"The surveillance. How much more than casual?"

"I don't mean that he had an army tailing him. Just one operator. On his other trips we just saw him aboard and made certain he arrived on time at his destination. This time we put a man in his pocket."

"A new man?"

"Why do you say that?"

"He didn't do a very good job," I said.

"No, not a new man. A good man with plenty of experience."

"So how did he let it happen? How did he let the hare fall or get pushed off the train? How come he didn't at least know about it?"

"Well, he did know about it."

"Is he the one who pulled the emergency?"

"No."

"Why not?"

"He was under instructions not to let our presence be known."

"Was he CI-three?"

"What do you know about CI-three?" Trask said. If he hadn't been sitting on the tombstone, I expect he would've taken a step away from me as though believing I was about to pull a knife or gun on him.

"For God's sake, Trask, the way you people act. Do you shred your laundry list? CI-three's common knowledge. Half the schoolboys in America say, 'You be SMERSH and I'll be CI-three' when they play spy and counterspy."

He got off the tombstone, smiling in his sleepy way, and I knew he wasn't taking my kidding too well.

"A friend of mine read about CI-three in a magazine," I said quickly. "Don't take it so goddamn serious."

"Well, it is serious, Hatch. Don't you know it's serious? Foreign agents are sucking up the industrial secrets and technology of this country like a bunch of vampire bats. Sucking the country dry. Keeping the bastards away from military secrets is the smallest part of it."

"Are you CI-three?"

He grinned. "I come and go, come and go."

"If you wanted to stay out of it when those bodies took the tumble out of the train, why are you getting into it, now?"

"We didn't expect anybody to go as far as you've gone, Hatch. We expected it'd just be chalked up as another accident along the right of way. That somebody'd finally come to figure that two lovers were playing grab-ass in the deadhead car and didn't notice the door was open. But them getting chopped up the way they did kept you interested, didn't it?"

"And I'm still interested. How much of what happened did your operator see?"

"Wouldn't you say I've already given you more than you expected or deserve? Where's the tit for tat?"

"Do your people know that your Benjamin May was carrying a gate pass to some company in his wallet?"

"How did you find that out?"

"I tracked down the dead woman's boyfriend. They were both gypsies. Did you know that?"

"Oh, we got that far."

*I didn't think they had.*

"Well, she passed the wallet to her partner after she picked May's pocket."

"He showed you the wallet and its contents?"

"No. He said he got rid of everything but the cash that was in it."

"Didn't try to sell the credit cards?"

"Sold the wallet, credit cards, driver's license, gate pass, and all."

"You don't happen to know who bought it?"

"Sure I know who bought it. A guy calling himself Jackson."

"Calling himself?"

"He also calls himself Howard Freeman—"

Trask's eyes opened as wide as I ever saw them open.

"—and he's the coroner of Washington County, Colorado. Now you tell me what you know about Howard Freeman."

"What makes you think—"

"For God's sake, Trask, I'm not the enemy."

"That's what you say, but damn if I don't go crazy trying to figure out sometimes who's the enemy and who's not."

"Like Howard Freeman?"

"Freeman was an agent."

"For who?"

"For us. He worked for the agency. He was separated about two years ago."

"For cause? Was he a rogue agent? Was he dealing secrets?"

"Nothing like that. He was just an overachiever who was more than a little foolish. You know about that agent working out of D.C. got himself all tangled up with some Russian emigrée woman sometime back? Got her into bed while she was thinking she was getting him into bed? Lay there night after night screwing and trying to worm secrets out of one another? All the time the CIA has a tab on his ass?"

"I seem to remember something like that flashing by on the late news."

"Goddamn life's turning into a bunch of flip cards," Trask said. "Well, that bugger, without telling anybody, set up the whole operation on his own. Wanted to stick in his thumb, pull out a plum, and say, 'Look what a good boy am I.' Well, Howard Freeman tried to pull the same thing locally."

"Have we got Russian emigrée lady spies running around the prairie?"

"I told you the action was with industrial secrets," Trask said. "Between Denver and Chicago there must be fifty companies with government contracts that hardly anybody knows about. Everything from chemical and metallurgy firms to ceramic engineering and computer companies. Freeman thought he'd found himself a foreign agent. It turned out she was a looney tune who liked to fuck a lot and play let's pretend. He was let go without prejudice because they figured he was just a romantic—you know he ran away and joined the circus once?—without any real harm in him. He begged for another chance and said he'd follow orders like a good soldier from then on but the whole thing had been a big embarrassment to the agency and they separated him anyway. Now it looks like maybe that wasn't such a good idea."

"You think Freeman took what he learned working for the agency and went into business for himself?"

"It's certainly starting to look that way."

"You know, Trask, this is a lot more than I expected you to give me."

"Well, Janosky and I talked it over—"

"I figured."

"—and decided we should be generous to an old friend and colleague."

"Am I going to be a colleague?"

"We'd like you to be. We'd like you to help us get the goods on Freeman if there're any goods to get."

"What did you have in mind?"

"Well, we'll just have to think on that, Jake, and if you'd be so kind, why don't you think on it too?"

## Twenty-eight

*PING-PONG BALL. GEORGE had called me a Ping-Pong ball. I felt more like a chicken running around with his head cut off. If you've never actually seen such a thing, it's hard to imagine just how awful it can be.*

I'd said a quick good-bye to Harriet, dropped off the rental car, and made it to the station in time to catch the nine o'clock to Akron. I walked the train, saying hello to Halt and Billy and Laws, then my legs gave up on me and I took a seat.

Halt sat down with me outside of Fort Morgan.

He put his shoulder satchel on his lap and a woman's brown leather pocketbook on top of it.

"You taken to carrying a purse, Laws?" I said.

"Picked it up under a seat back there. Didn't belong to anybody in the car. Probably left behind some other time and the cleaners missed it when they went on through. I'll just turn it in to lost and found."

"What do women carry in their pocketbooks nowadays?" I said.

"How should I know?"

"Well, let's take a look. Got to find out who it belongs to anyway. If she doesn't come looking for it, lost and found could give her a call."

He pulled things out one by one and laid them on the seat between us. It made quite a pile after a while.

"Comb. Lipstick. Compact. Toothbrush," Laws said. "Dental floss. Change purse. Wallet."

I nodded off while he was going through the inventory.

When I came to, we were pulling into Akron. It was almost 11:00 P.M. I stood there wondering if it was too late to call Maggie Wister. I called George instead and said I wanted to talk if he wanted to talk. He said come right on over or should he come and get me. I said I'd walk.

The same orange cat picked me up, looked at me with his knowing eyes, and left me at a corner.

I saw the light on in the kitchen when I reached George's house so I went and knocked on the side door. Bess let me in.

George was sitting at the kitchen table drinking coffee.

"That stuff will keep you awake," I said.

"I want to be kept awake," he said.

"Oh, then, if it's no trouble, I'll have a cup and stay awake too."

"Help yourself," Bess said, sitting down as though wearied by her pain.

"Why don't you go to bed?" I said.

"I will, in a little while."

"Everything all right in Denver?" George said.

"G-men were at the morgue to officially take over the case."

"They were here too."

"I know. Trask told me they wanted to make sure you didn't miss the message."

"That Janosky," George said, and made a sour face.

"That was one of the ones gave me my orders to mind my own business. Then the other one, Barry Trask, a man I've known for some time from Omaha, fed me some information. Told me the man who was killed under the wheels was a foreign agent."

"Now, why would he do that?"

"Because he wants me to help him put the bee on Howard Freeman."

"You'll have to run that train by me one more time," George said, hunching nearer.

"Why, for heaven's sake," Bess exclaimed, "Howard lives right here in Akron. He shops at the same stores. He's the coroner."

"Well, let me tell you, Bess," I said, and proceeded to lay out my surmises on the table.

I told them how Freeman had been so hard to raise because he said he was out to the barn with a sick cow, except he had a farm that didn't show hide nor hair, nor sign nor sound, of any cattle, even though he'd told me a story lately about not using one barn but another. "I've got a feeling that if we go over to his farm we won't find any cows, sick or otherwise, in that barn near the house."

I went on to say that Freeman had claimed he couldn't get near the train because the bridge across the stream on the vehicular road wasn't safe, and there was no other way to get there. But there was another road, a fire road, along the ridge, paralleling the track.

"It's more than possible that a man wouldn't think of a fire road as a way of getting anywhere in a storm like the one we were having that night," George said.

"I'll give you that. What I'm saying is that it's a road that could've been used to get from the train to Akron if someone pulled the emergency right at the spot where it was pulled and got off the train."

"That'd mean somebody'd have to have a vehicle waiting."

"That's right."

"They'd have had to know that they were going to get off the train at that spot. That they *meant* to get off."

I nodded and laid out the next sequence. How Freeman had risked a quarrel with George over searching the body while Freeman was there to see. How later on he'd asked me if anything else had been found when Bosley did the autopsy and then how the change was stolen from the envelope in George's office.

"Well, there goes your theory up in smoke," George said. "If Freeman was standing right there going through their possessions with us, why would he have to take the trouble to break in and steal a handful of change later on?"

I pulled my handkerchief out of my pocket and untied the corner one more time. I laid the nickel on the table. It sat there giving off an oily sheen. "Maybe because he didn't know what he was looking for the first time. Then he thought it over and figured there was more than one way to carry information than on film or on a piece of paper."

George gave his little grunt that said he wasn't buying yet, but was still willing to listen to the rest of the pitch.

I mentioned that Freeman had asked me one more time about what might have been found on the body after the rest of the woman was found.

Then I told him about the apparition Jim Tiptree and Halt Ennery had seen waving what looked like a sort of a cross made of metal around and how I'd found the metal detector in Freeman's barn.

Then I told him how I saw Freeman buying a wallet from the gypsy kid.

"There's something you can just go up and confront Howard with," Bess said.

"And he looks us in the eye and says he was over to McCook for this reason or that, stopped into a diner for a cup of coffee. Some peddler sells him a snakeskin wallet. If the gypsy says otherwise, Freeman looks him in the eye and calls him a liar. Who's anybody going to believe, a gypsy or a county official, duly elected?"

George looked at me like he was studying my nose.

"You've got a powerful collection of speculations," he said. "But the meeting with the gypsy's the strongest thing you've got, and with a little effort, that can be explained away. We really don't know much of anything. We're just speculating. Not even that. More like gossiping."

"That's not all about Howard Freeman," I said, and went on to give them chapter and verse about his career in the FBI.

When they'd exclaimed sufficiently about that, I

reminded them of Trask's offer for me to help the FBI get the goods on Freeman.

"One more thing," I said.

George looked at me, frowning like an old boar.

"Somebody's got to go out on that mountain right of way again."

"What the hell for?"

"Bess said something about it, but we just let it breeze by."

"What's that?"

"The girl's purse. She was wearing tailored slacks and a jacket with just one little pocket. Her purse should be out there on the slopes. If it's not . . ."

"If it's not?" George said, too impatient to wait for me to drop the shoe.

"Then it's something we're just going to have to invent and say we found out there."

A car roared into the backyard. George was on his feet and at the window and I was right behind him.

Dan Crack came tumbling out of the cruiser, moving faster than I thought he could. George was through the mud room and had the door open before his deputy got his foot on the first step. I stood in the doorway of the kitchen while Crack gasped out the news. "I just found Annie McMonigle huddled up in the doorway back of the office. She's dead."

# _____Twenty-nine_____

ANNIE WAS CURLED UP in the doorway like Crack'd said. And sad to say, she reminded me of a shaggy old hound lying there, just as Bess had feared.

George and I squatted down and gently pulled aside the layers of sweaters and scarves loosely covering her neck and face.

"I uncovered her a little looking for a pulse," Crack said. "But I put her clothes back pretty much like they were."

"You did all right, Dan," George said, standing up. He stood there looking down at her, a sad expression on his plain Scots face, the nearest thing to mourning I expect he'd ever show until the time, God forbid, when and if Bess was taken from him. "What the hell was she doing sleeping in doorways in weather like this? She had a house."

"I guess she didn't like it much," Crack said.

"She had plenty of warm places to sleep when the weather got cold. Plenty of cellars and furnace rooms and sheds." George sounded angry. I guess he was angry, a little, at Annie for living her life and dying her death in such a stubborn, independent way.

"Couldn't we lift her up off the cold ground?" Bess said.

"Unlock the door, Dan," George said.

"It's open." Crack opened the door as George and I stooped down to pick up Annie. Rigor mortis hadn't set in, despite the cold, and we were able to straighten her out before we lifted her up and carried her into the office where we laid her on the couch.

Bess set a pillow from the couch under Annie's head and folded her hands on her breast. Then she went to get a throw blanket from a cabinet.

Annie's mouth had a little lipstick on it and her cheeks, a little rouge. She'd painted her fingernails. A few were broken. They peeked out of her fingerless wool gloves like peeled twigs. She hadn't done a very good job but I wondered why she'd bothered to do it at all. A piece of nail was snagged in the wool of her topmost sweater. I picked it out and stuck it in my pocket.

"You ever see Annie gaudy herself up like this before?" I said.

"Women like to feel pretty every now and then, no matter what their age," Bess said as she put the cover over Annie. She didn't cover her face, though. Annie's eyes were closed and she looked like she was sleeping.

"I'm here," Freeman said as he walked through the door.

George had called him from the house saying,

"We'll do everything by the books, Freeman. Just like you like it."

Freeman took off his gloves and went to kneel beside Annie.

"Not unexpected, is it?" he said. "Could have happened any day."

Everybody uh-huhed. What else was there to say?

Freeman was fiddling around Annie's neck. "Only thing is . . ." I could hear it coming. "She didn't die natural. Somebody broke her neck."

Freeman stood up. George and Crack knelt down to have a look.

Freeman had a distressed look on his pudding face. I stood there looking at his face for signs of guilt.

*But what reason would Freeman—what reason would anybody—have for killing old Annie?*

"What are you staring at?" Freeman asked.

"Sorry. Just thinking."

"Oh? How's that?"

"We found out who the young woman was."

"You did?"

"Oh, yes. She was a gypsy pickpocket who worked the trains and platforms between Chicago and Denver."

"That's something."

"They work in teams, you know. I tracked down her partner. A young fella named Nick Kemp."

"That doesn't sound gypsy."

"Oh, the name's just a lie they use with the rest of us."

"Where'd you find him?"

"Over to McCook."

192

"I didn't know there were any gypsies living over to McCook."

"You know much about gypsies?"

"No, I just meant I thought they lived in the big cities."

"Kemp lives in Denver."

"So what was he doing in McCook?"

"Beats me. It all just happened lucky, me making the connection with him. In a diner it was. You know the diner across the street from the railroad station in McCook?"

"I haven't had occasion to go to McCook very often and when I did go there I didn't notice any diner across from the station. But I suppose there's a diner across from every railroad depot in the country, isn't there?"

"It was just one of those lucky chances," I said. "I was over to McCook asking did anybody see a young woman hanging around the station early in the morning. I had the purse we found along the right of way with me and—"

"What purse?"

"When George found the rest of the girl's body down along the river, he found a lady's pocketbook too."

"Why didn't I get to see it?" Freeman asked, his voice rising in agitation.

"Take it easy," I said.

He looked around and saw George and Crack watching him. Bess was standing at the foot of the couch watching him too.

"You're making too much out of the authority

you've got as coroner. You're second potato to the sheriff no matter how you slice it. Besides, there was nothing much in the pocketbook and George and I decided it might not be a bad idea for me to take the purse along with me when I took the rest of the body back to Denver."

"How's that?"

"In case anybody could identify it along the way."

"You said you were in McCook. That's the opposite direction from Denver."

"I went to Denver. After I went to McCook. I had an idea, so I went there to ask a few questions. That's when I got lucky about Kemp. See?"

"I still should have had a look."

"Well, don't you go taking the trip to Denver to have a look," I said, "because the pocketbook's not there anymore."

"Where is it?"

"I sent it to Nick Kemp care of that diner over in McCook. When he identified it as his girlfriend's, I told him I'd do my best to get it back for him and that's where I'd send it."

"Something like that could get lost in the mail," Freeman protested.

"I didn't mail it. I put it on the eleven-o'clock train."

"The eleven o'clock's heading west and McCook's east."

"I know that. But the train comes back again, don't you know. The pocketbook will be at the diner by two o'clock tomorrow morning—not this morning coming but the one after actually—and the gypsy boy can pick it up there when he pleases."

The wheels were turning in his head.

*Was he wondering if I was the fella who stepped into the diner and stepped right out again? Was he thinking that I saw him and was jerking his chain for the fun of it before telling him that I knew he'd been sitting with the gypsy?*

"Where'd you come off doing a thing like that?" he said.

"It was no big thing, Freeman. I just wanted to do a little something for a poor fella who'd lost his sweetheart."

# Thirty

ONCE WE WERE QUITS of Freeman and back in the kitchen having coffee at McGilvray's house, George said, "What the devil was that story you spun for Freeman all about?"

"As Sitting Bull said just before Little Big Horn, 'I saw my chance and I grabbed it.'"

*Which was fine, except that now I had to contact Nick Kemp and guarantee his cooperation, get Trask and maybe Janosky to agree to it, hope that Freeman, though a wary old trout, was hungry enough to snatch at the bait, and see if Maggie Wister thought she'd be able to do what I hoped she could do.*

"Well, it was just about as complicated a bunch of comings and goings as I ever heard. By way of accomplishing what?" George said.

"You happen to know how Trask left town? Did he go in Janosky's car or what?"

"Janosky left him to find his own way home and went back to Denver. Trask asked him would he drop him at the Donut Shop so he could get a bite to eat and have a place to stay warm until the eleven o'clock pulled out for Omaha."

"Do you think you could take a run down there and see if he's still hanging around? Maybe I can give him reason to stay over one more night."

"Well, aren't you going to tell me what your grand scheme's all about?"

"No reason to chew my cabbage twice. You go fetch Trask and I'll tell it once for the two of you."

"And me?" Bess said.

"I surely wouldn't leave you out of it," I said as George went to get his coat and limped out the door.

"Can I use your phone?" I said.

"It's right there on the wall," Bess replied.

I punched in the number the gypsy youngster had given me. After a long time a woman's voice came on. When I asked for Nick, she told me there was no Nick living there but in case there might be a Nick stopping by what should I say I wanted to talk to him about.

"You just tell him it's Jake Hatch."

Kemp got right on.

"I'm not saying the fella who calls himself Jackson around you had anything to do with actually killing your sweetheart, but I've got to tell you there's reason to believe he's committed some serious crimes against the country. What I want to ask you is are you willing to do what you can to help us get the goods on him?"

There was a long silence on the other end of the line.

"I can hear you counting up the costs and figuring

the profit, Nick. I don't think that's the right thing to do. Your sweetheart's dead and I'm ready to do what I can to get her things back to you. Things you might want to keep as tokens. Stop thinking there's you and then there's us. Do what's right and never mind the profit."

His voice came over the line as though it was clogged with sand and glue. "What do you want me to do?"

"Somebody'll deliver a lady's pocketbook over to the diner in McCook. That'll be around two o'clock in the morning. We'll make sure the diner's open. Right after two we want you to go in and get the pocketbook. Take it over to that corner booth next to the big plate-glass window. The one where you were sitting before. Understand?"

"Yes."

"Go through it like it was your sweetheart's and the things in it are dear to you. When Freeman comes in—"

"Who?"

"I mean when this Jackson comes in—if he comes in—you say that it's Cara's purse when he asks you."

"How do you know he'll ask me?"

"If he goes to the diner and talks to you, he'll ask you about the pocketbook. Believe me. So you tell him it's hers. He'll ask to look through it. You tell him like hell. You don't want any stranger pawing through your dead sweetheart's belongings. Then he'll probably offer you money just to have a look. Act suspicious as hell—"

"I *would* be suspicious as hell anybody asked to do something like that."

"You bet. Then you start acting shrewd. Tell him you want to know why a man would pay good money to look in a girl's handbag. What we want is for you to get him to say right out that what he hired you and Cara to get from that other fella could be in that bag. You say that unless he tells you what it is he can go scratch."

"He's a big man. Suppose he just decides to take the bag away from me by force? Will I be clean if I take a knife to him?"

"Don't do that. For God's sake, don't do that. Just let me say that you won't be alone. Somebody'll be close by. You got all that?"

"Yes, I've got it."

"Say it back to me."

He said it back to me practically word for word.

I'd scarcely hung up when George was back with Trask in tow.

"Sit down and let me tell you what I have in mind," I said.

I reviewed for Trask's benefit what I'd said down at the sheriff's office when Freeman had come to have a look at Annie's body. Then I told them both about the arrangement I'd made with the gypsy.

"That sounds like a fine idea," Trask said. "Well, it would be if it goes off like clockwork. Except for one thing."

"What's that?" I said.

"How do you expect us to get close enough to bear witness to anything that passes between the gypsy and Howard Freeman?"

"The Widow Wister," I said.

# _____Thirty-one_____

THE WHOLE BUSINESS, FROM the instant the emergency cord had been pulled at 4:20 A.M. on a cold, pitch-black, rain-lashed right of way along a spine of lesser mountains, through the finding and delivery of the body parts to Akron that morning; and the day lost getting up the search party that went out and found the other half of Bela Mazurky, AKA Benjamin May, that night; and me getting my ear clipped before I transported the rest of him back to Denver and Bosley's care; and then going back to Akron, snooping around Freeman's farm, putting up storm windows, hearing how George McGilvray had plucked the other half of the girl out of the river and me taking her back to Denver with a stop in McCook along the way where I lucked out about Freeman and the gypsy youngster; and the discovery of poor old Annie McMonigle, until the minute when a small crowd of us were gathered in the waiting room of the station in McCook, had taken more than five days but just short of six.

*I felt a hundred and ten years old, give or take a year.*

George had come along even though he had absolutely no authority and could participate in no arrests so far out of his jurisdiction, in another state let alone another county. Deputy Dan Crack had asked to go along to be there when the son of a bitch who'd murdered Annie got caught, but George'd persuaded him that it'd be a lot better if he stayed at home and minded the store because with his temper—Crack was as mild-mannered as a pup—there was no telling what he'd do to the killer if he lost it.

Trask had called down to Omaha and had three men from the field office there flown to McCook and Janosky flew four along with himself over from Denver.

The local chief of the constabulary had to be informed about what was going down in his bailiwick, so Chief Charlie Ogden was there with three of his officers.

Maggie Wister was sitting next to me on a bench. She was the calmest woman I knew—I'd scarcely ever seen her do so much as lift an eyebrow at anything I ever told her—but I could tell that she was a little excited about the role she was going to play in this.

When they spotted the television reporter Karen Olliphant, both Trask and Janosky came to me wanting to know who she was and what she was doing there. We'd already made it up between us, when I got in touch with her at the motel, that we'd play it like we were strangers. I craned my neck to look at her, then asked them how the hell I was supposed to know what

201

a woman was doing in the waiting room of a train station with a train due to come through on the way to Chicago any minute. She winked at me behind their backs. Trask went over and asked her if she'd please inform him before going outside in case she got a notion to do so. She asked him what was going on, the way any curious bystander would do. He told her they were on a stakeout and she said, in a very sweet, innocent way that she'd always thought a stakeout was a lonely operation done by two or, at the most, four cops sitting in cars or working in the streets dressed like utility workers.

I went over and gave Cooley one of Bess's pocketbooks wrapped in brown paper. It had the usual stuff any woman would carry in her handbag. In the change purse, along with some nickels, dimes, and quarters was the plugged nickel.

Nick Kemp drove up and parked in front of the diner right on schedule. He went inside and we could all see him slide into the booth at the end. Cooley came out from behind the counter to get his order and hand him the package. They both looked over to the station as though Nick had asked where the man who'd delivered it had come from and Cooley'd told him. The gypsy took the brown paper off the purse.

The train going to Chicago pulled in and out around 1:53, right on the button.

The one passenger who got off looked at the crowd in the waiting room, wondering what the convention was all about.

Chief Ogden went over to him and said, "It's nothing, Jethro, just some Shriners passing through. Go on home and think nothing about it."

Jethro just nodded and went out the door. But he didn't go home, he went directly across the street to Cooley's and climbed onto a stool at the counter.

"Chief Ogden," I said, "I think it might not be a bad idea if you strolled over to the diner and told Jethro not to mention the crowd hanging around the station." I raised my voice a little so everyone would hear. "And if I were the rest of you, I'd go into the station office, the toilets, or back up against the wall. The man we're expecting used to be an FBI agent and he'll surely still remember how to brush his coattails."

There was a lot of shuffling of feet as they lined up like ducks along the walls. Ogden went to the door. George, who was stationed at the window that looked out on the street, said, "Here comes Freeman in his pickup." So Ogden had to stay.

I got a pair of compact binoculars out of my pocket, handed them to Maggie, and moved her to the window at an angle so she could see into the diner across the street without being seen. I had another pair for myself. I tapped her shoulder so she'd look at me.

"You need help with the focus?" I asked.

She threw me a glance as though I wasn't very bright, then went back to looking.

"Is the stenographer who takes sign ready?" I said.

A skinny FBI agent wearing two sweaters came over with a pad and pencil ready and leaned against the wall so he could watch Maggie's right hand like a hawk.

Inside the diner I saw Nick Kemp pour water on the seat on the other side of the table, just like I'd told him to do. Fifteen seconds later, after standing on the step and looking around very carefully, Freeman went inside. I could see him make a beeline for the gypsy. He was about to sit down when Kemp pointed. Just as I'd hoped, Freeman didn't bother mopping up the mess but just shoved in alongside Kemp when the youngster slid over and made room. So they were both facing our way and Maggie had a fair to good look at both their mouths.

Her hand started flashing. The stenographer's pencil flew. He spoke as he wrote.

"The boy says:

'Hello. What the hell're you doing here?'

'I was just about to ask you the same thing.'

'I came to get a package that was left for me.'

'Oh, is that so? What kind of package?'

'This was in it.'

'Looks like a pocketbook.'"

I could see Freeman open the pocketbook and start going through it. Kemp started to protest but Freeman shot him a look and the boy thought differently about it. Maggie went on. "The boy says:

'It was Cara's.'

'Now, who'd give you something like that?'

'It was found on the train. She must've dropped it. My telephone number was inside and some nice person in the crew called me. I asked them to drop it here.'"

*This was a sticky part.*

Maggie signed and the stenographer said out loud, "Freeman says:

'Why would you want them to deliver it to you here?'"

Kemp didn't say anything for a couple of seconds. Freeman had opened the change purse and was pouring the coins out on the table. He turned his head toward the youngster, a suspicious, inquiring look on his face. Then, clearly, something dragged his attention right back to the coins. He picked one of them up. I knew it was the nickel.

"Freeman says:

'Well, what the hell do you know about that. Why the hell not. Who needs the formula when you can steal a sample?'"

He jerked his head up then, looking toward Jethro, who was talking to Cooley. He half stood up, his hands supporting himself as he leaned closer to the window, looking across the street right at us, looking sharper now for the crowd of cops and men gathered in the railroad station that Jethro was gabbing about.

"The rabbit's on the goddamn run!" I shouted, and headed for the door, jerking it open just about the time Freeman got into his pickup and slammed the door. He was racing off while the rest of us were still jammed up in the doorway like a bunch of Keystone Kops.

# Thirty-two

FREEMAN LOST US ON the dark roads right from the starting gun. By the time we got all unscrambled and settled into the various vehicles standing by, he was probably at McCook's city limits. Anyway, the McCook police decided to drop out of the chase about the time we hit the Red Willow County line.

When we crossed the state line into Colorado, I could only see one of the two cars loaded with FBI following George's cruiser with Maggie, Karen, and me in the back.

"Where do you think they're going?" George said, glancing in the rearview at their headlights.

"I'm willing to bet you a dinner they're just following you."

"Well, where the hell am I going, Jake? It looks to me like the bird has flown."

"I don't think so, George. I think he's making a beeline for his farm."

"Now, why would he do a dumb thing like that?"

"To get his hands on a couple of things he's got there, for one thing," I said. "And because he's not really on the run for another."

"I can't see how you figure that."

"Well, I could be wrong, George, but I don't think I am. No use talking about it till we get there. If it's all right with everybody, I think I'll have myself a little nap. Will you wake me when we get to Freeman's farm?"

Before George could say any more, I closed my eyes.

*I wondered should I lean my head to the left and rest on Maggie's shoulder or to the right and rest on Karen's. I decided to let my head fall forward while I pondered that.*

I woke up to the sound of George's tires braking on the gravel drive alongside the farmhouse's side door. I had a crick in my neck so bad it was giving me a headache. A few gulps of cold air sliced off the top layer or so as we unloaded ourselves from the car.

Trask, Janosky, and two agents drove in behind us.

We all stood around looking at the house. Every window in it was lit.

"He doesn't look like he's hiding," I said.

"He could be ready to make a stand," Janosky said.

I cleared my throat because I didn't want to bust out laughing and strolled over to the kitchen door. I didn't even bother knocking, I just walked in.

There was a big pot of coffee simmering on a new

electric range. The swinging door to the parlor was open and I could hear music coming from inside. I walked in with the others right behind me.

The first person I saw was Millie from the Donut Shop, all dressed up like she was going somewhere, face painted and hair freshly done. She was sitting in a club chair with her ankles crossed and a drink in her hand, trying to look nonchalant, though the little smile on her lips trembled a little.

Freeman had changed into a suit, shirt, and tie. He'd combed his hair. The smell of Vitalis was sharp. He was grinning like a cat.

"Put your hands flat and empty on the table," Janosky said.

Freeman did as he was told and said, "Who's your friend, Barry?"

"You really stepped into it up to the neck this time, Howard."

"What're you talking about? It's about time for you to break out the citations and the medals."

A car pulled up outside.

*The other carload of FBI hadn't gotten lost after all, I thought.*

Freeman moved one finger. "There's this," he said, pointing to a small card, "and then there's this," pointing to the nickel.

I went over, picked up the card and read it. "Prentiss, Martin and Davis."

"Metallurgists," Karen said.

The front door opened.

Trask looked at Karen sharply and said, "I thought you caught the Chicago train."

"Oh, no, I thought I'd come along and see the rest of the excitement."

"This is Karen Olliphant," I said.

"Newspaper?" Trask asked.

"Television," Karen said. "We'd be into it sooner or later."

Trask was about to say something more when Dixie Hanniford came into the living room from the hallway. She wasn't dressed in her rough clothes but in a nightdress and dressing gown. Nothing flannel, only silk and satin with a stylish trenchcoat thrown over her shoulders. She was even wearing feathered mules.

"What the devil's going on here? You all right, Howard?"

Janosky reared back and said, "I'm going to order all unauthorized persons to—"

"Oh, can it, will you Janosky?" I said. "This movie's just about over. All the actors are here now and I want to get to the end of it."

Freeman looked at me.

"Freeman got wind that this foreign agent, Bela Mazurky or Benjamin May, had stolen information out of the factory of a firm, located between Akron and McCook, that formulates new alloys," I said.

"For the government," Freeman said.

"He decided he'd pull the chicken away from the fox right out from under the nose of the wolves—"

Freeman grinned at Trask and Janosky.

"—so he hired a couple of gypsy pickpockets to pull a switch and get him Mazurky's briefcase on the train."

*What I was going to say next wasn't true and I knew it.*

"He discovered that the information he'd paid to have stolen wasn't in the briefcase. He went through the train and found Mazurky and the gypsy girl, Cara, in the deadhead. They were—"

"No!" Freeman yelled. There wasn't the trace of a grin or a smile on his face. "I never went looking for anybody. I wasn't even on the train. I was right here in Akron down by the station. When it was late by an hour, I went on back home."

"You didn't struggle with the two of them? They didn't fall out the door under the wheels? You didn't pull the emergency right there and jump off the train?"

"If I'd done anything like that, how the hell would I manage to get back to Akron in time to come down to look over the bodies?"

"Well, you weren't back in Akron when the dispatcher called and talked to Millie, were you?"

"I was at the station."

"When did you realize Mazurky might've been carrying the goods in some other form?"

"I knew that metallurgists cast sample slugs. I figured one of them could be mixed up in the change in Mazurky's pocket. I never figured somebody at the laboratory would cast the slug to look like a nickel."

"What were the marks on the nickel?" George said.

"Test impacts. Different marks for different times in the process of casting, stamping, and annealing."

"So if you didn't pull the emergency, who did?" George asked.

"The person who killed Mazurky and the gypsy girl," I said. "The person who murdered Annie McMonigle."

They all looked at me.

I was looking at Dixie Hanniford.

# Thirty-three

FOR A MINUTE THERE, with just about everybody staring at me wide-eyed and openmouthed, I started hoping for a hole in the floor to open up and swallow me. What I had to go on was so small, an intuition would've looked like a certainty beside it. I thought I had the ends figured out, but I surely couldn't lay down chapter and verse about the means.

"For God's sake, Jake," Trask said. "There's the guilty man sitting right there with his finger on the reason why he did what he did."

"His finger's on the evidence," I said, "but what he did wasn't killing."

Dixie started laughing and set herself down in an easy chair, head thrown back as though trying to get a clearer view of this madman who was posing as a railroad detective.

"What Freeman did was a lot of romantic foolishness," I went on. "He was kicked out of the agency because he went off half-cocked, a case of too much misdirected enthusiasm. It figures he'd do something harebrained trying to redeem himself."

"Hey," Freeman said in protest, but that was all he said. He wasn't so foolish as to interrupt the man who was trying to save his bacon.

I looked at Millie. "Or maybe he just wanted to show off a little for Millie after they got to be good friends."

"He didn't have to impress me by doing anything special," Millie said in a small voice.

"So Freeman was down around the depot, keeping out of sight, waiting for the train to pull in so he could retrieve the briefcase his hired thieves had stolen, when the dispatcher called looking for the coroner. Millie was in his house. I'd guess she often stopped by in the morning to spend an hour with Freeman before she had to go and start opening up the Donut Shop. She told the dispatcher the first thing that came into her head. The business about the cow."

Dixie stole a look at her hands, to see, I suppose, if she had herself under control. Her nails were manicured and enameled. She caught me looking and folded her hands in her lap.

"Freeman wasn't even on the train, but Dixie Hanniford was," I went on. "She was on the train because she wanted what Bela Mazurky had even more than Freeman wanted it. Mazurky was working for the same crowd she was working for. They had suspicions that he was doing a little business on the side."

"With me," Freeman said. "Nothing important at first. It only cost me nickels and dimes."

"Which would be a good investment when Mazurky finally offered him something big enough to get Freeman back in the bureau's good graces."

"I didn't have the money for anything important."

"When that time came, he'd already decided he'd steal it. All this time, Dixie was bird-dogging Mazurky and saw Freeman make contact. She figured Freeman for the key. When he made his move, she knew Mazurky'd be making his move. She came to live in Akron so she could watch Freeman better and easier."

Dixie coughed as though she had some congestion, putting her hand up to her mouth to show how delicate and feminine she was.

"I can't give you every dip and two-step, but I can describe the dance," I said. "I figure Mazurky caught wise that somebody'd pulled the switch on him on the train and figured out it had to be the young couple who'd jostled him. He went looking for Cara, who'd decided to play it safe and finish the journey in the deadhead. I don't know if Dixie knew what he was looking for—I doubt it—but she followed him into that empty car ready for a confrontation. Mazurky was in the middle of forcing a confession out of the gypsy girl. Dixie joined the struggle."

She laughed then. It sounded like the yip of a small dog. She tossed her head around as though she were having difficulty controlling her mirth.

"The size of the man," she said.

"A man with emphysema who had to struggle for breath after the slightest exertion. The fight didn't last long. Mazurky and the girl were both shoved out the door."

"Are you saying the deaths of Mazurky and the girl were accidental?" George said.

"No. Cara's death wasn't planned. She just happened to be there when Mazurky was scheduled to get his. Dixie Hanniford—or whoever she turns out to be—was on that train to kill him. She had a vehicle waiting for her over the gully and ridge on the fire road. She pushed Mazurky and the girl off the train. Then she pulled the emergency and got off herself. One side door being left open by accident I could accept, but both of them being left that way was more than I could swallow."

Dixie stood up. I couldn't help noticing what a fine figure of a woman she was as she arranged the coat on her shoulders and held the wide lapels closed across her breasts with her red-tipped fingers. "I came over to see if I could help a neighbor who might've been in some distress," she said. "I can see he's in no danger. I enjoyed the entertainment. Now I'm going home."

"I don't think so," Janosky said.

"I haven't heard anything substantial, have you?" she said. "Bedtime stories. All I've heard have been complicated bedtime stories."

"Taking a shot at me was no bedtime story," I said. "Killing Annie McMonigle was no bedtime story."

"Now, just why would I have done anything like that?"

"It was you I interrupted in the sheriff's office going through the property envelopes. You knew what you were looking for but you didn't know the plugged nickel wasn't in with the change but in my pocket. You took a shot at me and got the devil out of there. But Annie, who curled up in the back doorway of the sheriff's office sometimes, saw you. . . ."

"Or saw Howard looking for the same thing," she said.

"Freeman is the coroner. Annie wouldn't think it very strange to see Freeman in the sheriff's office. He was a county official. She'd have no reason to think he was doing anything illegal. But she knew that you'd have no right nosing around there in the dead of night. She came to ask you what it'd be worth to you for her to mind her own business. You showed her how much it was worth."

Dixie huffed and started for the door, but Trask stepped in front of her. She turned around to face me again.

I took the scrap of fingernail from my pocket. "This was caught in one of Annie's sweaters."

"One of her nails," Dixie said.

"Now whatever would make you say a thing like that, Dixie? Poor Annie's got polish on her poor old broken nails, all right. It's the same color as the polish you've got on yours. You put it on her after you throttled her because you noticed one of your own nails had been broken off in the struggle and you didn't know but what somebody'd find it and wonder where it came from. If you take a look, Trask, I think you'll find that one of Dixie's perfect fingernails is one of those artificial ones they make out of plastic."

Trask took one of her hands. Dixie didn't pull away. She just looked at me and called me something in a foreign tongue. I knew it was no compliment.

# _____Thirty-four_____

THE NEXT DAY MAYBE fifty people from the town gathered to see Annie McMonigle to her rest.

Howard Freeman and Millie were there. They'd have to work out with Calvin what would have to be done now that their affection for one another was public knowledge instead of common gossip.

Dan Crack stood beside the grave with watery eyes, staring down at the plain pine box as though counting his own days.

Maggie Wister stood beside me, composed and silent.

George was there with Bess.

She'd washed Annie's face over at the undertaker's parlor and let the undertaker do the rest. She'd put a quarter-ounce gold eagle in Annie's hand. When George'd asked her where it'd come from, she told him Annie had given it to her for just that purpose.

The minister of the Unitarian church said a prayer. Maggie said her own in sign.

When it came time for the toast by name, according to the custom of the gypsies, we all looked at one another, wondering how to handle it.

Bess stepped forward and said, "Godspeed. May the long road be short. Godspeed, Esmeralda Estremadura."

After the graveside service, those who wanted to went over to the McGilvrays' for something to eat.

That evening I stayed with Maggie Wister.

But I was gone by ten o'clock so I could catch the 10:56 back home to Omaha.

# Red Cent

My name is Jake Hatch and I'm a detective for the Northern Burlington Railroad which runs between Chicago and Denver.

Believe it or not, I've been on trains on several occasions when someone's taken a shot at it.

The railroad crosses the Des Moines River just west of Ottumwa, about sixty miles south of the Sac and Fox Reservation in Tama County, Iowa. Unhappy Indians occasionally remember Sitting Bull and ride out at dusk in Jeeps or pickups to make their protest against the "white eyes" by shooting at the iron horse.

So when a passenger, having his dinner in the dining car, got shot through the temple, most people thought it was just an extraordinary and regrettable accident, but I found reason to believe it was deliberate murder.

**Watch for *Red Cent* by Robert Campbell,
coming soon from Pocket Books.**